Rarity MOUNTAIN

Love, Hope, and Faith Series

JOURNEY TO FAITH

Sara L. Foust

Silver Living
Literary Services

©2019 by Sara L. Foust

Published by Silver Lining Literary Services, LLC
106 Offutt Rd.
Clinton, TN 37716
www.saralfoust.com

Second edition. Printed in the United States of America

First edition printed in 2019

ISBN 978-1-7329047-7-4

Cover by Diane Turpin at dianeturpindesigns.com

Scripture quoted are from the King James Version of the Bible.

*And now abideth faith, hope, and charity,
these three; but the greatest of these is charity.*

I Corinthians 13:13 (KJV)

Chapter 1

Dr. Fern Strongbow settled into a folding chair across the desk from Dr. Sylvia Greenlee. Fern popped a flower into her mouth and smiled as her friend and mentor grimaced. "Dandelion?"

Sylvia shook her head. "You eat some strange things, Fern."

"They're delicious." Fern ate another yellow top and smiled. "What's on the agenda for our weekly session?"

A dog whined in the next room, drawing Fern's gaze to the office door. No doubt Max was having trouble awakening from his dental surgery. Pentothal did some strange things to their patients in recovery.

"I'm sure Kaylee can handle that."

She was probably right. But what if Kaylee was otherwise occupied? Fern leaned back into the cold metal and sighed. "I miss the old chairs."

"Well, they were worth $50 at the farmer's market. Paid the water bill last month."

Max whined again.

Fern's gaze once again darted to the closed door. "You sure Kaylee isn't busy with something else?"

"Max will be fine. We need to talk."

Sylvia's gaze landed on the wall behind Fern's head instead of greeting her head-on in that penetrating, straightforward way Fern had come to appreciate long ago. Strange. Did she have more news about the clinic? Fern's pulse skipped.

"As you know, things have been tight around here. But I haven't been completely honest with you about how bad things are."

Fern's stomach flip-flopped. Her chewing mouth stopped. "Oh?"

"I know I promised you partnership in another nineteen months, but we aren't going to make it that long."

Wait. What? Her pulse swished in her ears, thumping like the poor dog's tail against his crate-prison in the next room. "What are you saying?"

"As of today, I'm seeking a buyer for the clinic. I'm sorry."

Words ping-ponged around in Fern's mind, but none of them found her mouth. She swallowed the bitter flower.

"You'll be fine, Fern. You're a survivor."

Her neck stiffened. "Survivalist. There's a difference. We've discussed it a million times."

"I mean it. You are a survivalist, but you're also a survivor."

No, she wasn't. She was a mess inside. Barely keeping it together so no one noticed. Where would she go now, with her dreams of part ownership in Knox Highway Veterinary Clinic dashed? Her safety net yanked away, feet dangling over open space, a chasm of uncertainty yawning below. How could she remain in control when everything was being turned upside down?

Simon Fincuff returned his attention to the strips of flooring. Not a hard floor to lay, but one that required his best work, considering the customer. Arnie reminded him of that every morning when they arrived.

Mrs. Golden's nasal squeak sounded from the other room. Growing louder with each word.

Upset again. Why didn't that surprise him? Was it his imagination or did he hear her spit out his name?

Arnie's muffled argument ended with the slam of a door.

Simon glanced up as Arnie entered the room, reading the words on his boss's face before they formed on his lips.

Arnie shook his head. "I'm sorry, man."

"Not your fault."

"It's different this time."

Simon's motions froze. The next words coming, the sentence forming in Arnie's mind would change everything, wouldn't they? Again.

"I've got to let you go, Simon. She insisted. I'm sorry."

Heat burned Simon's cheeks. "Not your fault."

"She did a background check of her own, you know. I didn't tell her."

"I know."

"If I have another job, I'll call you."

Yeah, that's what they all said. Once he'd been let go, he never got that follow-up call.

Simon gathered his tools and tucked them into his canvas bag. He didn't say goodbye to Arnie or the job site. No one would miss him after a few days passed. Why couldn't people see past his past? Yes, it was dark, but there was light underneath. One he wanted to shine brighter than the penned ink of failure.

Another job lost. Another uncertainty looming. What was he supposed to do now?

"Come in, Betty." Gregory Vanderbilt, III, laid down his pen and took the chewed lid from his mouth. "Don't hover."

"Sorry, sir. I didn't want to interrupt."

"We do this every day. What exactly did you think you were interrupting?"

"I don't know, sir. Sorry."

Gregory held out his hand. "List."

Betty's hands shook as she gave him the clipboard.

She wouldn't last another week. He'd bet money on it. "This is all of them?"

"Yes, sir."

"Buy. Pass. Buy. Buy. Pass."

"Sorry, which ones?"

"Good gravy." He picked up the pen and scribbled in the margins. Buy veterinary clinic. Pass putt-putt course. Buy television station. A good buy, that one. Buy the gas station. With an overhaul of its front appearance, it should be profitable. Pass on the bank. He owned enough banks already. Well, his dad did anyway.

Gregory thrust the clipboard into Betty's hands and waved her out.

The Knoxville Sunsphere's copper sides glittered under the gaze of a late summer's sunset. Would Pops be satisfied with his purchases today? How would he react if he wasn't?

Fern slipped her key in the lock, jiggled it, and swung open the front door. Hard to believe she would be leaving this place soon. A cacophony of barks, whines, and thumps greeted her.

"Good morning, furry babies."

Max yelped his reply. She would miss him the most. Most clinics had resident cats. Max loved the attention of being the sole resident dog. But he would go with Sylvia. Fern sighed and knelt in front of his cage. "Hey, bud, want to get out of there?"

His tail wagged in a blur of motion.

Fern massaged the soft spot behind his ears. Tears pooled in the corners of her eyes. No. She wouldn't let them come. Kaylee would arrive any moment. Fern couldn't let her see weakness. She'd lose the young girl's respect. Lose control. Max would be fine with Sylvia. And Fern had her own pets to console her. What she needed to focus on was finding a new place to work with a mentor as kind as Sylvia.

As Fern exited the rear door with Max, Kaylee stepped from her car and flashed a smile. "Good morning."

"Morning. I need you to get started in the kennel right away. Some of the animals are out of water."

Kaylee's smile fell. "Yes, ma'am."

Kaylee didn't need Fern's prompting, but Fern couldn't help herself. Issuing directives was an easy way to avoid small talk. Avoid intimacy with subordinates. With everyone. Kaylee may not like her much, but Fern preferred dislike to disrespect any day.

Sylvia pulled into the parking lot and waved. "I've got news."

Already? Fern's stomach turned cold.

"We've found a buyer."

How could Sylvia's tone be so upbeat while Fern's chest ached so?

"Deal closes Friday. We have to get on the phone

with clients now and refer them elsewhere. Find new doctors to transfer care for the inpatient ones."

Fern narrowed her eyebrows to a painful crease. She wanted to argue. To say no. Would it do any good?

"I know this is hard, Fern. But I could use your help. I know you want to make sure these guys are cared for."

"I do." There were those dumb tears creeping in again. Why? Why did they have to show up today when they hadn't been a part of her eyes in so many years?

Gregory leaned against the hood of his dark gray Mercedes, crossed his arms over his chest and his legs at the ankles, and waited. Always waiting, wasn't he? Waiting for Pops to arrive. Waiting for Pops to leave.

Waiting for Pops to approve.

He shook the last thought from his mind with the flick of his hand and the recrossing of his feet. The television station proved to be an interesting acquisition. Whether Pops liked the idea or not. Jenny would've understood his desire for this project. Too bad he hadn't seen her in ten long years. Wonder what she was up to? She was married, Gregory knew from a weak moment of Facebook stalking a few years ago. To a man whose smile seemed genuine and tattoos proclaimed a touch of hippy in his blonde-haired, free spirit. Good for her.

He could see his cheesy movie now. He would be wearing the typical director's hat, the silly-looking thing with a bulge above the forehead and the bill at the back. Holding a megaphone and yelling orders from the linen-backed chair loudly pronouncing DIRECTOR in bold script. A smile curved the corners of his lips. Could he really make it happen? Finally use his psychology minor to put into play the dream he'd held since he was a boy?

Except it wouldn't be a cheesy movie. Maybe a game show. No, a wilderness survival challenge. Ooh, that was good. Setting player against player in the most extreme situation he could muster, and watching them struggle to survive, striving for the grand cash prize.

It would need to be somewhere remote. Somewhere challenging, yet full of natural resources—

"Son."

Gregory's daydreaming snapped out of view, replaced by his father's scowl.

"I've spoken once already. I shouldn't have to speak twice."

"Yes, sir." Gregory took his father's carry-on bag from his outstretched hand. "How was the trip?"

"Good. Bought that warehouse dirt cheap. It was on its last leg, so they didn't have any room to negotiate."

As usual. His father swooped in, snatched up the struggling, and dug in his talons.

"What have you accomplished while I was

away?"

Ah. There it was. Time for the inspection. And it had only taken four point five seconds for him to ask. A new record. "Acquired several businesses." Gregory opened the door for his father.

"I assumed that." He sat in the passenger seat and aimed his gaze out the front window. "Details, son."

Gregory shut the door a bit harder than he should've and made his way to the driver's seat. "I bought the veterinary clinic and the gas station."

"Good, good."

"And a television network."

His father's silence yelled at him. Was he ever going to respond?

"Sell it."

Chapter 2

Fern crossed her legs and uncrossed them. Crossed them again. Folded her hands in her lap and took a deep breath. Could it really have been a week already? They'd rescheduled all the appointments and transferred care to a veterinary clinic in Fountain City. All the animals were taken care of. Max with Sylvia. Kaylee at another clinic. Sylvia on an extended vacation. Fern alone.

The door opened behind her. She forced a smile and turned to greet the office manager.

"Sorry about that." He returned her smile and sat at the desk. Straightened his tie and slid papers from a file.

"I understand. It's a busy day."

"Yes, well, let's get right to it. I've looked over your file. You graduated in 2013 Summa Cum Laude. Very impressive."

Fern shifted in her seat.

"But you only have four years' experience, in one vet hospital. I'm afraid what we're looking for right now is . . . Someone with more varied experience." He rose from his chair and extended his hand.

She flinched. Robotically rose to meet his grasp.

"Thank you for coming in."

All that preparation fixing her hair and changing outfits five times. Calming her nerves and driving with shaking hands. For less than five minutes of face time. And a rejection. Couldn't they have called her to tell her no thank you?

Fern forced herself to nod. "Thank you for your time."

She let herself out of the office into the plain lobby. The receptionists ignored her as Fern stooped at the water fountain. She raised her head and swiped the back of her hand across the drops at the corners of her mouth. Her fingers froze. A blush crept onto her cheeks. So close she almost bumped into him, a man with a thick brown beard and piercing eyes waited for a turn at the fountain. "Excuse me."

"Take your time."

Straight, white teeth cut through the brown, and his face was transformed. Handsome. Striking. Her pulse skittered away from her normal self-reserve. She slipped past him and almost ran for the door. When had she last noticed a man in this way? Not since that night had she looked upon the male sex with anything but scorn. They were all deceivers. Selfish manipulators. She needed to force these current emotions into submission, but her heartbeat didn't seem to agree with her.

Simon chuckled as the beautiful woman skirted for the door. He hadn't meant to frighten her. In fact, he was dressed nicely for a change. Trimmed his beard and everything. Showered. Brushed his hair, though it did need a trim. Surely he wasn't such a scary sight?

"Mr. Fincuff?"

"That's me."

"I'm ready for you now. Right this way."

Simon followed a shorter man in slacks, dress shirt, tie, and loafers to a small rear office with no windows. Not a very practical outfit for a man working with animals all day.

"Have a seat."

"Thanks." He settled into the armed chair.

"You are applying for a kennel position, I see."

"That's correct."

"Do you have any experience in this field of work?"

There it was. The question. The question everyone asked and seemed to put so much importance on. "No, sir. I am a skilled floorer but have never worked at a veterinary hospital."

"Why the sudden interest?"

Desperation made men do all sorts of unexpected things. He cleared his throat. "It's time for a change, sir. I may not have experience, but I am a quick learner and good at taking directions."

"Well, while the kennel position doesn't require specific degrees and such, we do prefer candidates with at least some experience. Have you ever owned a pet?"

"I grew up with dogs and cats, sir."

"Yes, well, thank you for your time. I will keep your file and let you know once I finish interviewing all the candidates."

Simon rose first and extended his hand. "Thank you. I'll look forward to your call."

He escaped the stuffy room before the office manager could reply. Simon wouldn't hold his breath.

Back outside where he could breathe, Simon unbuttoned his tight collar. The image of the woman at the fountain played in his mind. Her long, black hair had been pulled straight back so tight he wondered if she got headaches. But there was something about her. About the way her almond-shaped, Jacobean eyes reminded him of the color of his favorite flooring. He would most likely never see her again. But he wouldn't soon forget her.

Behind Gregory, the heavy door swung shut with a loud click. His footsteps echoed down the empty hall.

Where were the light switches? He felt his way along the wall until his hand struck an eight-switch panel. With an upward sweep, he turned them all on at once. Fluorescent bulbs fluttered to life, casting a bright yellowish glow over the entire building. The television station awoke in a quiet jumble of dusty desks, piles of equipment, and cameras on tall stands looking forlorn and forgotten with their faces pointed toward the floor.

Gregory's chest swelled at the thought of the possibilities.

Sell it. Humph. This one time, just this once, he was going to have to disobey his father. He had tucked the information about this acquisition into a corner of Z Enterprises he hoped his father would never check. Maneuvered some unpurposed money around. Covered his tracks fairly well, he might say. It wasn't like Pops did any of the accounting himself anymore anyway.

He would need to buy more equipment. Some smaller, motion-activated cameras with live-feed ability. And outdoor protective stuff for the gear. Whatever it was called. He'd learn about that as he went. Maybe he should hire someone who knew these things. That way he would free up his mind for the creative angle. His college roommate, Turner, would be perfect. Last Gregory had heard, Turner was free for hire, working freelance and not getting many gigs. He'd probably be happy to have some work and lend his skills.

So much to do. Thankfully, Pops was leaving again in the morning. This time for two weeks. That should give him plenty of time to interview players and get the filming started. Gregory rubbed his hands together and then whipped out his phone. "Betty?"

"Yes, sir?"

"Copies ready?"

"Yes, sir."

"Great. Meet me at the curb in twenty minutes." He would post the flyers himself. It had been a long time since he'd done something as menial. He flipped off the lights. A lilting whistle escaped his lips.

When was the last time he'd felt such enthusiasm spark?

She might as well have one more cup of the good coffee while she still had some money in her savings. Right? Fern slid into a patio chair at Old City Cafe and sipped her white mocha. A man in a light suit stepped in front of a car on the small side street. The car honked, but the man smiled and waved. He continued to bounce toward the cafe with a handful of flyers. She stifled a giggle. What in the world was he so happy about? He must not be worried about job hunting or paying bills.

He stopped at the cork board and pinned up a colorful paper, whistling as he pushed the thumbtack in.

There was something about him that held her attention. Though he was handsome, it was the grin that fascinated her. He returned to his dark Mercedes and sped away.

Fern grabbed her coffee. She had to see what he posted.

Calling all Survivalists! A great opportunity to audition for a new television series. Survival Tennessee. Show up at 202 Market Street Friday, July 7th, 2017, ready to exhibit your skills. Prize money? $500,000 each.

Her eyes widened. Half a million dollars? Was she meant to see this flyer today? Had some fate of the universe placed her here at exactly the right time, with exactly the right skills, with exactly no career? She pulled the bright purple flyer from its pinned home, folded it, and stuck it in her pocket. Two days from now a different sort of interview awaited her.

Simon scanned the board filled with flyers of all different sizes and colors. Old staples held tiny strips of torn paper like announcement confetti. Concerts on University of Tennessee campus. Special deals on textbooks and CDs at McKay's. Roommates wanted. Pet sitters available. No job postings. It had been a long shot, he knew, but he was getting more desperate. Two more "no thank-you" interviews this week. No returned calls. No leads.

A bright green flyer in the corner caught his eye. A survival challenge? With a huge prize? Now that could prove promising. What did he have to lose at this point? He was a talented hunter and camper. At least he had been before . . . He shrugged. Skills like that were like riding a bike, right? Surely old experiences would count for something. And if he spent the next two days watching YouTube videos on survival skills, maybe he could bluff his way through the interview process. It was worth a shot.

He jotted the address down on the back of a business card from his wallet.

With $500,000 he wouldn't have to worry about any more interviews. About the call backs that never came. Wouldn't have to worry about his past that never left him. He could start fresh. Maybe move far away, like Alaska. Somewhere no one knew him.

But what about Lance? His younger brother was sinking into their pasts. Burying himself in guilt. How could Simon leave when he was the only one who knew the real truth? The only one who could protect Lance.

Gregory chewed on the blue pen lid as he read over the questions his new team had compiled from his dictations over the past twenty-four hours. He had woken at least a dozen times during the short night to record slurred but exciting ideas into his phone. Not to mention the morning hours spent letting his imagination run wild.

Five young interns squirmed in their seats around the marble-topped conference table.

"All right. Let's get started. We don't have much time. Intern number one," Gregory pointed at the woman directly to his left, "you will be sitting on the panel with me. I want detailed notes of each person that comes to try out for the show. But I don't need your input, so silence will be expected." Was it callous he hadn't bothered to learn the interns' names? Maybe, but it didn't seem necessary. They'd only be here until auditions were complete. And he was paying them handsomely. He moved around the table clockwise. "Number two, you will be at the door as participants come in. You will hand them a copy of these rules." Gregory held up a thick stack of papers. He'd stayed up late into the night typing them. Not his secretary. Him. He raised his chin a bit higher. "You will also need to ensure we have enough copies made ahead of time."

"Yes, sir," number two answered.

Ah, one of them did have the courage to speak to him. Surprising. "Number three, you will be charged with making sure auditioners are separated and kept that way as long as they are in the building. I don't want them talking to the ones still waiting." He didn't need the other two. "Four and five, you can go home."

The five interns exchanged wide-eyed glances. Four and five raced out of the room.

"I will need you each to sign this nondisclosure agreement. It absolutely forbids you to speak of the interview process, the questions, the television rules, et cetera. Under no circumstances will it be tolerated should I hear that you have leaked information to anyone, family included. You will face criminal charges." He took a moment to lock gazes with each one of them. Hopefully, it would be enough to keep everyone involved quiet. And keep word from ever reaching his father. "You three will be here at seven o'clock tomorrow morning. Understood?"

They nodded.

"Copy room is down the hall to the right."

When none of them moved, Gregory resumed munching on the lid and turned his chair around to gaze out the window. The interns shuffled papers and feet behind him as they left the room. But he was already miles away. He needed the perfect pair of contestants. Ones who had skeletons in their closets they were terrified would come to light. Ones who would be skilled survivalists but also push each other's buttons. The only way a TV show of this type, this tired, overdone type, could stand out from the rest was if it was different. And different meant conflict. Lots of it.

Gregory dialed Turner. Their conversation had gone well the day prior. "You ready?"

"All set. I looked at your video equipment. I need money to purchase more, man."

"Done. Come by today and pick up my Visa."

"See you in an hour."

Everything was falling into place. Turner in

charge of filming and hiring the few members of a crew. Interns helping with auditions. And he was scouting locations this weekend. As long as he could keep Pops in the dark, his plan was coming together. A couple more days and Gregory would take his show far away from the offices of Z Enterprises. And, if all went according to plan, the first time Pops would hear of it would be when the debut episode aired. Piece of cake.

Chapter 3

Fern swung open the tall glass door, sending a shaft of ice-cold air past her shoulders into the sweltering morning. Waves of heat radiated from the pavement over downtown Knoxville. The lobby of Z Enterprises, covered in glass and cool metal sculptures, wasn't necessarily inviting. The deep red color of the reception desk added little to its hospitality. Fern's resolve wavered but for a moment before she bolstered her confidence. She was the most competent candidate, no doubt. Her childhood primed her for such an adventure as she faced now. How many backwoods East Tennesseans could say that?

The receptionist greeted her with a smile that didn't reach her eyes.

"I'm here to audition. For the survival show."

"Nineteenth floor. Take the hall to the right."

Fern nodded. This was it. A half-million would

buy her very own veterinary practice. She pushed the silver button and waited while the elevator hummed and slid open. Red carpet and pale lights overhead made the small space feel claustrophobic. Soft music played, doing little to temper her nerves. Just stay in control of the conversation. Stay in control of yourself. She took a deep breath and let it out slowly. The doors slid open silently, ushering her into a wide hallway.

A woman with a clipboard stopped her outside a set of large, wooden double doors. "Name?"

"Dr. Fern Strongbow."

"Take this packet and read over it. You can wait over there."

The short brunette directed her to a waiting area filled with plush chairs and magazines. The walls were covered with massive photos of a silver-haired gentleman shaking hands with all sorts of professional-looking people. She didn't recognize any of them. But she got the impression she was supposed to.

Was she early? She double checked her watch. Nope. Why was no one else waiting for an audition?

Maybe it was all a hoax? And she was a fool.

But if it was a joke, the receptionist would've laughed. And Fern wouldn't be holding a mini-novel on her lap wondering what she'd gotten into. She flipped open page one and began reading.

Rules of Survival Tennessee. Please read thoroughly. If you are chosen and accept a position as contestant, you agree to abide by the following rules:

1. Both contestants must complete the challenge

together in order for the prize money to be awarded, $500,000 each upon completion.

Both contestants. She'd have a partner? Why hadn't that occurred to her before? She could control her own actions but not those of another person. And that person would have the chance to make or break her odds of winning. This was a bad idea. She couldn't survive with someone else. Too much outside the bounds of her control.

Fern jumped from her seat. If she could make it to the elevator, she could sneak away, and no one would know what a clown she almost made of herself.

"Dr. Strongbow?"

The deep voice behind her made her wince.

"We are ready for you now."

Smile. Act like somebody. You can always decline later when they offer you the gig. Fern took a deep breath and turned. "Thank you."

A young man with glasses led her through the doors into a spacious conference room. The table stretched long between her and what she assumed was an interview panel. Like a barrier of judgment. And stern frowns. And loads and loads of serious glares.

A gentleman in a dark suit and colorless tie spoke first. "Thank you for coming. I am Gregory Vanderbilt, creator and financier of the show. This is Turner. He's in charge of the filming crew. We'll get right down to brass tacks, as they say."

Fern sat in the lone chair on her end and took in the attire across the table. Gregory's outfit spoke of wealth, seriousness, power. Turner, though, in his t-shirt and slouching shoulders told her he was a bit more laid back. She'd bet he wore shorts and flip-flops under the dark table. Who was the quaking wisp of a woman to the left? Probably unimportant. She needed to direct her smiles to Turner, her business tone to Gregory. She may no longer want the position, but she wouldn't appear the fool she felt she was.

Gregory stuck a pen lid in the corner of his mouth. "Tell us why you are qualified to appear on the show. I assume you read the instructions."

She had barely had time, but she couldn't show weakness. "I am a veterinarian. I was raised on an off-the-grid homestead. No indoor plumbing. No electricity. I spent the first seventeen years of my life hunting, butchering, and preparing meat. Building shelters, starting fires with bow drills and flint. Tracking. Sleeping under the stars. My mother was an expert at edible wild herbs and plants, and she passed that information down to me. I doubt you'll find a more suitable candidate."

"We will judge that, Dr. Strongbow. Though I am impressed with your background. What skills can you demonstrate for us today?"

What? She'd not planned to improvise outdoor skills in a tall, stiff building nineteen stories above ground. She glanced around and cleared her throat. "Anyone have a pocket knife?"

Turner produced a yellow-boned folding blade from his pocket and slid it across the table.

"See that box?" Fern pointed with the opened blade to a blue plastic tote marked recycling.

The gentlemen nodded.

With a flick of her wrist, the knife flew across the posh space and sunk deep into the box's side. "I can procure food in the wild. Easily."

"Impressive. We have several other candidates. We need you to fill out an extensive questionnaire, medical release, medical history, and permission to request prior medical records. Once you finish those, we have more questions. We will give you twenty minutes to read over the materials and fill out forms."

Medical history? How far back would they check? Surely they couldn't get those records. They were sealed because she'd been a minor.

"You can be excused."

"Thank you." With legs that quaked a bit, she returned to the still-empty lobby and began leafing through the papers. She hadn't expected this. Why had she dreamed she would march in, talk a bit, and walk out with a role? Of course they had to protect themselves in case something happened. And she didn't even know what to expect on the show. Wait. Was she considering saying yes now? Would she get a chance to ask questions?

Maybe she should go home. Mr. Vanderbilt's actions belied his words. He hadn't been impressed with her. Rude. Belittling. Not wowed.

And did she want him digging around in her past? Exposing the details she fought to hide from everyone? She began to read the instruction packet.

Are you in a relationship?

Why would they need to know that? No.

Can you leave for thirty days or more?

She guffawed. Yep. Nothing to hold her anymore.

Do you have any debilitating fears that would prevent you from finishing the challenge?

Debilitating? No, nothing she couldn't handle.

Do you consider yourself a loner or a team player?

A loner, but could she put that and still have a shot at being chosen?

She read the reminder at the top of the sheet again. "Honest answers are required. We will pull details of your past."

Loner.

The questions went on for the length of the page, followed by a medical disclaimer, which she signed, excluding Z Enterprises, Gregory Vanderbilt, III, and the television show from indemnity should she sustain injury or die.

Die? Her heart skipped a beat. She should leave. Get up and walk out. Why was she still sitting in this comfy chair, answering these crazy questions?

The dream she'd had the night prior came back to her again. Cycling around and around, the image of her own practice. Run her way. No chance of being "let go." No boss. She could be in control of every aspect.

The next page included the medical history release form. She tapped her pen on the clipboard. If she gave her current primary care doctor's name, that's all from whom they would request records. Right? She scribbled her signature.

She filled in the questions about her major medical histories and issues. None. As far as she knew, she was in perfect health.

Now, to read the show details in more depth.

Participants will be challenged by a series of questions, tasks, and puzzles in order to earn survival supplies and find the prize, which will be hidden somewhere nearby. Cameras will record every minute of the challenge and be watched live by a team of behind-the-scenes crew members. If participants are suspected of lying or cheating in any manner, supplies will be removed. On top of the challenges imposed by the show's producer, participants must also fend for themselves in the wild and survive for as long as it takes to solve the riddles and find the prize money. Don't think this will be a short stint, an easy task. It won't be. Prepare yourselves for a month's stay at minimum.

A month?

Survivalist participants will be given the opportunity to bring two items with them to begin and have the chance to earn a number more.

There will be wild and dangerous animals. Bears, bobcats, elk, and venomous snakes. There will be someone watching you at all times, but you will be alone with your partner most of the time.

Alone with her partner. What if it was a man? What if she couldn't stay in the alpha role?

Half a million dollars to each participant is waiting somewhere. Tucked away. Hidden. You won't find it without the clues. Don't even try.

The money. So tempting. So life-changing. She could handle anything this Gregory guy chose to throw at them, as long as her partner could.

She signed the bottom of the page without reading the rest of the booklet. It didn't matter what it said. Her mind was made up. She was going to win that money. And prove to the world she was capable of this challenge. Or drive her partner crazy trying.

He held the door for a slim blonde with disappointment streaking her mascara. Simon smiled politely, but inside he hoped that it meant less competition for a spot.

Once he exited the stairwell into a plush lobby on the second to highest floor, he was directed to a small room with a coffee pot and a few chairs around an octagonal table. No other contestants?

Good. He'd brushed up on his skills as best he could yesterday, but if the audition required him to demonstrate fire making or shelter building, he'd be sorely under-prepared.

He leafed through the thick document presented

to him by the clipboard woman. Nothing too surprising. They'd delve into his past. Like everyone. Would his record knock him out of the running here too? No matter what that cruel file said, he wasn't a bad guy. He'd prove it today. Turn on all his charm. Fire up the big words dictionary in his mind. Impress the loafers off those TV gurus.

He read through the rules and signed the proper places.

"Simon, we are ready for you, sir."

"Wonderful." He added a smile to the bubble he hoped shone through in his voice.

In the conference room, he slid into the chair, folded his hands on the table, and aimed his attention on the gentleman opposite making introductions.

"We have an extensive list of questions for you. Are you ready to begin?"

"Fire away." Pun intended.

"What do you feel is the most important quality in a partner?"

"Dependability."

"What are your unique talents as they pertain to this type of show?"

Simon renewed his smile. "I grew up hunting and fishing with my dad. We camped a lot. I learned primitive skills from him early on. It's been a little while since I've had the opportunity to use them, but I look forward to breaking them out once more." He probably shouldn't have said that last part.

"Do you feel two people in a relationship should

be honest about their pasts?"

A relationship? Like a partnership, they meant. Surely. "Yes."

"Good, good. Are there any secrets you would never share?"

Yes. One. "No, sir." They could never know that truth. No one could. But it wouldn't affect some television show or Simon's ability to survive in the wild, so it was a nonissue. No reason to even begin to dive into it.

"Good to hear. If cast on the show, you will be put to the ultimate test. Physically and mentally. How would you rate your ability at solving riddles and puzzles? On a scale from one to ten."

"That's a hard question to answer. If it involves a math problem or logical thinking, I'm very good. I've spent the last several years laying flooring. It requires precise measurements and an eye for patterns, like fitting together puzzle pieces."

"Any objections to working closely with a woman, alone, for an extended time period?"

"No, sir. I'd look forward to it." Simon winked, which earned him a smile from Mr. Vanderbilt and Turner. He figured it would.

The questions continued for another half an hour, ranging from skills and abilities to preferences in partnerships.

"One last question, Mr. Fincuff. Are you single?"

"Why does that matter?"

"We want to be sure your family ties would not

prevent you from completing a long stay in the wilderness. Homesick. Missing family and all."

"I'm single, sir. I may miss my parents and brothers, but not enough to leave the challenge prematurely."

Mr. Vanderbilt and Turner exchanged Post-It notes.

"Very well. We will take your completed forms and let you know if you make the final cut."

"Thank you. How soon should I expect to hear something?"

"Tomorrow."

"Wow."

Mr. Vanderbilt raised his eyebrow. "We need to move quickly on this project. Will that be a problem for you?"

"Not a problem at all." Maybe this one time, he'd hold his breath. Just a little.

The sun's evening rays bounced off the Sunsphere and lit up the conference room. Gregory's favorite time of day. Beautiful. And he had the quiet office to himself and his own pursuits. "Well, Turner, what do you think?"

"I think you've had a lot of eager people in here today. Hard to tell which ones are being honest about their abilities without testing them."

"Oh, I can tell." One of his specialties, reading

people.

"All right, so which ones weren't feeding us a bunch of bologna?"

"Simon, Timothy, Anders, Jolene, Katelyn, and Fern."

"Six out of twenty-five?"

"Yep."

"My favorite of the men was Anders. Women was Fern. That knife flinging of hers could really help her out there. Both with the critters and her partner, if you know what I mean." Turner's coarse laughter filled the room.

"I liked Fern too. Something about her. Let's put her on the final list for the women."

"Agreed."

Gregory munched on a lid. "Not sure Anders would make a good partner for her, though."

"I thought you wanted drama?"

"I do. But not the sort that would make. He'd antagonize her all right with his macho attitude. But I don't think they'd get past that to mesh well enough to complete the show."

"You don't want them to fail? I thought the point of this was to create good television."

"Failure doesn't equal good television. Just shorter filming and a disappointing ending for an audience. Trust me. I know what I'm talking about."

"That whole psychology degree mumbo jumbo stuff again?"

"Precisely."

Turner crossed his leg over the opposite knee and leaned back. "Did your dad ever find out about that psychology degree of yours?"

"He doesn't need to know. How about Timothy?"

Turner chuckled and held up his hands. "Fine. We won't talk about your dad now. Or ever. Like usual. I liked Timothy. Talented with outdoor abilities, it seemed. If you're right, and he wasn't bluffing."

"He wasn't."

"You make the calls first thing in the morning. I'll pack the gear and we'll get up there to scout the location Saturday."

"Excellent."

Turner padded from the room humming a Jimmy Buffett song.

Things were coming together well. Pops would be home in a few days and by then, he'd be "on vacation," filming on location from his director's chair. Would the candidates survive the way he hoped? Would they be a good match? He grinned. What a surprise they were in for once the challenges started. They'd think he was trying to kill them. Perfect.

Chapter 4

A part of Fern missed the homestead. The quiet mornings filled with bird songs rather than television jabber. The evenings reading books by flashlight rather than answering text messages. The solitude she could find the instant she skipped out her back door and slipped into the forest. She missed that the most.

Her small back yard, though she had planted a garden and hidden a little bench under the willow tree, didn't drown out the city noises nearby. The indoor bathroom was nice, though. And the hot showers. And her microwave after a long, exhausting day at the clinic.

The clinic. She frowned. Would she know more of those rewarding days any time soon?

She put her Camry into park, opened the door, and inhaled the onion-spicy scent of fresh mown hay. Her dad hailed her from the tractor mid-field. She returned the wave and watched as he turned the corner out of sight behind a peninsula of tall pine trees. If he seemed surprised by her visit, she couldn't tell from this distance.

Her mother's soft voice singing a good morning song to the garden drifted around the house. Fern smiled. She missed that morning song too. It played in her head most mornings, but it wasn't the same. "Hey, Mom."

Her mother's gaze snapped her direction. Wiping dirt from her hands onto her jeans, she rose and embraced Fern. "It's been too long, baby girl."

"I would've called, but you know." The old joke made them both laugh.

"Hard to call with no phone. I know, I know." Her mom squeezed her to her hip and guided her toward the porch. "Come sit with me a while. Tell me all that's new."

Fern's phone jingled in her pocket. Such an ordinary sound out in the world. So incredibly out of place here. "Sorry. Hang on a sec."

"I'll pour the lemonade and meet you on the front porch."

"This is Dr. Strongbow."

"Fern, this is Gregory Vanderbilt. You're in."

Her heart jolted. "Really?"

"We will begin Monday morning, seven o'clock sharp. I'll send a car for you."

No question of whether she'd changed her mind. Probably a good thing he didn't give her the chance.

Wasn't this what she'd asked for after all? "Okay great. Thank you."

"I'm emailing you now. You will need to choose from the list of allowed items only two to bring with you. Understood?"

Too bad she couldn't take more items. How would she manage with only two? "I understand. Do I get to know what my partner chooses?"

"Not until the show begins. We will be sure you don't duplicate."

"And what about my partner. Who is it?"

"That is also a surprise. You'll meet him Monday."

Him. Of course. Why couldn't any one do a survival show with a woman-woman partnership challenge? Had no one any original thoughts these days? "See you then." Man or woman, she wouldn't let it get to her. She needed this money. Wanted this prize. She would have to find a way to deal with it. She was strong enough now. A grown woman. She could handle anything.

Fern returned to the front porch and sat on the swing next to her mom.

"So, why are you here?"

"Couldn't I be here for a visit?"

"I suppose. Been a while since you did that though. Last time was to tell us you were moving. Time before that you had a new job."

"I do have some news."

"You're ready to come home?" Her mother's

eyes lit up.

"Not that. I have my own home now. Remember?"

Mom patted her knee. "This will always be home. You'll figure it out someday."

Would they always have this argument? "Mom. Seriously. Not right now."

"I forgot. This place is holding you back. What's your news?"

"Not holding me back, Mom." Fern sighed. She came today with the intention of warning her parents about her potential of being gone. Maybe getting a little feedback. But now that she knew for certain she'd made it to the show, she couldn't bring herself to disclose all the details. What if her mom tried to talk her out of it? Or thought she wasn't up to the task? "I'm going to be gone for a while. I took a new . . . position. It requires me to be out of reach for at least a month, maybe even longer."

Out of the corner of her eye, Fern could see her mom stiffen. "Will you be safe?"

Safe? Who knew? But had she ever been truly safe anywhere? Even on the homestead bad things had happened. "I'll do my best."

"What is this 'position'?"

"A survival challenge." Fern felt the speed of her words increase. She wasn't supposed to be justifying her decision, so why did she feel the defensive wall erecting? "I know it's been a while since I used my skills, but you and Dad taught me so many things. It's time I use them. I could win a lot of money."

"Humph. Money. You could be using your skills right here, Fern."

"This is your dream, Mom. Not mine."

"Your dream was to become a veterinarian. You did that."

Fern flew to her feet and crossed her arms tight around her chest. "I can have more than one dream, you know."

Her mom tugged Fern's hand loose and pressed it to her dirt-smudged cheek. "I just want my baby girl home and safe."

Fern softened. "I'll be careful, Mom. I promise. Maybe someday y'all will need a vet and my training will come in handy."

"When do you leave?"

Her fake smile fell a fraction of an inch. "Monday." Bright and scary. Could she keep herself safe with a strange man? With a wilderness filled with challenges and wild animals? She shivered. She'd take the bears and bobcats over the partner any day. Her sense of safety when alone with a man fell out the window the night she and Scott . . . Her survival tool number one would be a machete. And she wouldn't plan on sharing it.

The helicopter blades hummed overhead, blocking audibility if it weren't for his headphones.

Gregory peered through the oval window at the expanse of treetops below. "Rugged, eh, Turner?"

His friend's voice crackled through the headset. "You could say that again."

"It's perfect."

"I can't believe you bought all this without coming up here and looking first."

"I saw pictures."

"Forty-six million is quite an investment to make off pictures alone."

Gregory snickered. "Ever heard of a leap of faith?"

"More like a leap of fear of getting caught."

Gregory returned his attention to the scenery buzzing in swirls below them. Turner wasn't wrong. When Pops asked if he'd taken care of the television station problem, Gregory had said yes. But he didn't elaborate. How long could he keep Pops in the dark? And when it came to light, could Gregory keep his head on his shoulders?

Turner's low whistle drew Gregory's gaze to the other side. Gregory tapped the pilot on the back. "Land there."

The ground rose up to greet them, wind whipping the grasses of the small clearing in wild circles. "What is that?" Gregory tapped Turner and pointed to a collection of decrepit buildings at the edge of the grassy area. An old cabin, possibly? A barn too? Had someone actually managed to etch out a life here at some time in the past? Gregory and Turner grabbed their bags, stepped from the chopper, and darted to the edge of the meadow as the helicopter's blades slowly whined to a stop.

"What's the plan, boss man?"

"All we have to do is ensure some part of this area can sustain life. Find a water source and evidence of food. In 4,600 acres I'd be surprised not to find a suitable location." Gregory tightened the backpack strap around his torso. "Cross your fingers."

"What about the pilot?"

"He gets paid by the hour. He won't care how long we hike."

"Wish you were paying me by the hour." Turner grinned.

"You wouldn't miss this for the world."

"The adventure of a lifetime. Or the death of both of us. Your Pops is still a scary old dude."

Gregory wanted to laugh, but Turner was right. Unless Gregory proved the television station and his survival show could turn a huge profit, Pops would kill him. Or at the very least eviscerate him with words.

This was a terrible, terrible idea. Fern's tiny gear bag taunted her from the wall beside the front door. Nausea stirred her stomach. No way could she do this. That bag didn't contain enough to keep a dog alive for thirty days in the wild. Two survival items? Mr. Vanderbilt was insane. She pulled her cell phone from her pocket. Dialed with shaking fingers. "Gregory, yes, this is Fern."

"Problem?"

"Yes. No. Maybe."

"Well, which is it?"

A wave of discomfort shot through her lower abdomen. How could she explain? "I don't know."

"You're having cold feet."

"You could say that."

"I figured you were a woman of your word. Guess I was wrong."

Blood shot to her temples. Was he accusing her of being a liar? Or a weakling?

"The car is at your front walk now. Are you giving your half-mil away?"

Was she? Her pets were safely taken care of by Sylvia. Though Sylvia had drilled her with an onslaught of questions, Fern was sure of herself yesterday. What was wrong with her now? Her bills were paid. For the moment. There was nothing to hold her here. "I'm in." She clamped a hand to her mouth as nausea rose higher.

"Good girl. See you soon." Click.

Girl? How dare he! Once she got there, she'd give him a piece of her mind. If she could still walk on her liquid legs.

Gregory's phone jingled again. Better not be

Fern again. If she backed out, the show was over. None of the other women they'd interviewed could replace the element she brought.

"It's Timothy."

Oh. Great. "What?"

"I am . . . in an ambulance."

"Let me guess, you can't come."

"Medics think it's acute appendicitis."

"Wonderful." He hung up. Couldn't Timothy's dumb appendix pick a different time to rupture?

Simon.

Clearly, he exhibited skills. Compatible with Fern. He dialed.

"Hello?"

"You're up."

"Excuse me. Who is this?"

"Gregory Vanderbilt. Survival Tennessee."

"Oh."

"The helicopter will pick you up in thirty minutes."

Yes! Simon's heart skidded into overdrive. Someone had backed out and he was up for the chance of a lifetime. He sprinted to his bedroom, grabbed the small backpack. Paused. Was he ready for this? How long had it been since he'd been in the woods for longer than a few minutes? Three? Four?

He shook his head. Tied the bow to the

backpack's strap. Secured the arrows into the leather quiver. He was doing this. It was the best shot he'd had in years to overcome the stigma biting at his backside each second. He'd get away for a month doing something he loved and come home with a fortune. Easy.

Simon retraced his steps through the living room, and picking up his cell phone, shot his younger brother a text. **Mr. Reverend, Pastor, Brother Thomas, that opportunity came through. I will be out of town and unreachable for at least a month. Wish me luck!**

His brother's response dinged almost immediately. **Thank you, Mr. Smart Alec. Will do more than wish. My prayers are with you. Be safe.**

Simon snickered. Leave it to his little brother to remind him of the Lord in a moment like this. It was his job, after all. But Thomas meant every word, and even though they weren't on the same page, Simon could count on Thomas to do just that. **Keep an eye on Lance for me.**

He ran a hand through his hair. He should've gotten it cut before this. It wouldn't be very practical to keep up with out there.

Out there.

Where was there? And what was waiting for him when he arrived?

Simon flexed his biceps. Was he crazy for doing this? Mom probably would have said so. She didn't understand how much it hurt for her to treat him like he was a broken thing. He needed this redemption. He smoothed his beard. What difference did his hair make when his beard was as bushy as a bear's anyway? He chuckled and dropped his bag on the porch. His nostrils flared as he snorted out a breath, like the puff of a hot wind in the desert. What if he failed? His hands fell to his sides, slid into his pockets, twisted a quarter with his right fingers with each beat of his pulse. He couldn't fail. There was no redemption in failing.

Pursing his lips, he nodded to the audience of grasses and weeds in his front yard. Crossed his arms over his chest as the steady sound of the helicopter reached his ears.

A helicopter, eh? He'd never ridden in one before. Mr. Vanderbilt must have quite an income stashed away somewhere.

The uneventful ride zipped him over interstates, towns, and forests far below. A bit snug in the small cabin, but he managed to calm his racing heart as long as he kept his gaze glued to the scenery. As the Rarity Mountain exit loomed, the pilot began a quick descent that sent his stomach into his throat. A smattering of vehicles and clusters of people carrying cameras waited below.

This was it. Really it. He beat a rhythm in time to the chopper with his index finger on the opposing bicep.

The pilot signaled he could exit. He ducked and sprinted for the congregation of men with cameras. The magnificent view stopped him in his tracks. From their vantage point, with the interstate behind them, he could see for miles. Probably all the way to House Mountain. Nothing but mountains and trees and dense undergrowth. His knees nearly buckled. This was going to be his home for the next thirty days?

There would be plenty of wood to build their shelter. Ample rain from the common summer storms. Hopefully. He tapped the bow hanging at his side. And it hadn't really been that long since he'd used his hunting skills. They would be okay.

He scanned the cluster of people. None of them carried a pack like his. Where was his partner?

"Simon, great to see you." Mr. Vanderbilt extended a smooth hand and shook his vigorously.

"Thanks for this opportunity." Didn't Mr. Vanderbilt run a background check? Surely, the wealthy man had discovered his criminal past.

"Let's meet your partner." He turned and called over his shoulder toward a tan tent erected nearby. "Fern!"

A slender, dark-haired woman slipped from the tent. She raised diamond-shaped, Jacobean eyes to meet his gaze, and his heart thundered to life again, whisking away any hope of breathing.

Her.

Him.
It couldn't be. Fern's jaw clenched. The

handsome man from the veterinary office, with the densest beard she'd ever seen and the eyes like lights in liquid lamps. The only man that had caused her pulse to deviate in years. How could the universe do this to her? She pasted a smile on her lips even as her feet threatened to stumble.

"Fern, this is Simon. Simon, Fern."

Simon extended a tanned hand, fingers rough and split from hard use. She forced herself to shake it and contribute dialog to the conversation. What she said, she forgot as soon as the words escaped her mouth. A bead of sweat trickled down her back, tickling her spine. Adding to the quaking Simon caused within her.

She couldn't spend thirty days alone with him. Her body was already trying to defy her will. Traitorous heartbeat. Was it far too late to back out?

"Fern?"

The intensity behind Gregory's gaze brought her back.

"Are you ready? You look a little pale."

What a coward she was! The beauty of a section of the Royal Blue mountains stretched before her. Emerald, olive, sage greens rolling out before her like a bumpy carpet. A wind arose and brushed over her, bringing with it the scent of heavy rain waiting in the clouds above. The land would provide. The knife would be her protection. She was as ready as she could ever hope to be. She bristled and turned her attention back to Gregory. "I'm fine."

"Some last minute instructions. Listening?"

They nodded.

"Turner and his crew will be following you on foot until you reach a suitable point for camp. The ultimate decision is up to you. However, you will notice a set of pink flags. You are both not to go outside these borders. If you break this rule you will be sent home and forfeit the prize. Secondly, once you reach the place you want to make home for the next month, the camera crew will be rigging multiple motion-sensor, live-feed cameras. Do not attempt to move or tamper with these cameras. Here," Gregory handed them each a small camera, "are your personal cameras. I want detailed diaries from each of you."

Diaries? She turned the camera over in her hand. How detailed? Gregory couldn't possibly know her inner thoughts, so she could give as much "personal" details as she deemed fit. He'd never know the difference. She took a deep breath. Swallowed. Refreshed the pleasant look on her face.

Gregory turned to her again. "What two survival items did you choose?"

"A fire starter and a knife." Her knife.

"Good. And Simon?"

"Bow and arrows and a pot."

"Perfect. You two have chosen well. Remember, you have chances to earn more supplies through the Truth or Dare style questions that will be posed to you. Once you set up camp and settle in, you will receive your first clue. Some will be your responsibility to locate and solve, some I will send. Follow my rules carefully. I will be manning the live feeds from a distance. But keep in mind, someone is watching. And cameramen will be popping in from time to time. It is very important you abide by the rules as set forth in your packets. I assume you read them and memorized the dos and don'ts?"

She'd studied them. Internalized the important ones. Hopefully, Simon wouldn't be a rule breaker. Or dead weight. She didn't plan on carrying him through this whole endeavor. She could. But she didn't want to.

Chapter 5

Fern's gaze traveled the massive forest, mountainous terrain, and shimmering heat lifting from the treetops below. Was this really happening? She was crazy. Completely, totally nuts.

Gregory clapped his hands together. "Grab your gear and let's get this show on the road, as they say."

"Let me help you get your pack on." Simon smiled down from his lanky perch a head and shoulders higher than her.

"No. I'm fine." Was he already worried about her? That chivalrous junk wouldn't fly far with her. She could take care of herself. He'd see soon enough.

She returned to the tent, slipped her light pack on, and took a deep breath. She was doing this, but it wasn't her. It couldn't be. The real her was back at the clinic, treating cats and dogs for all sorts of ailments. Working toward partnership in a few short months.

This Fern, this part of her, died a long time ago. When she left the homestead, she had no intention of returning to stay. No need for her skill set in the city. Just a need for the locks on her doors and the solid bubble of Kevlar surrounding her heart.

Her body was moving mechanically, walking out of the tent, shaking Mr. Vanderbilt's hand, smiling as he wished her good luck, heart thumping against her breastbone, taking the compass in her hand and reading it. Blips of the past flashed through her mind, searing her emotions. Dark night. Parked car.

She was speaking, answering Gregory and Simon, but words came from somewhere subconscious. How did she know what to say at a time like this? More painful memories. Heavy weight. Screams of instant regret inside her head. No voice left.

Her legs, carrying her onto a faint game trail. Shady underneath. Relief from the pulsing sun rising over the eastern mountains. She watched herself from a squirrel's perch, it seemed, looking down on her own body entering this challenge. Inside shouting, "What are you thinking?"

Simon's hand, warm on her shoulder, gripped her. Squeezed.

The forest zoomed into focus, like a trick of a camera. The opening of a movie panning in from outer space. Fern shook his hand free and shuddered.

"You okay?"

The concern in his voice splashed over her,

comforting and irritating at the same time. "Uh, yeah." She took in her surroundings, noticing them in detail for the first time since entering the protection of the trees. "Wondering what we've gotten ourselves into, I guess." Not a complete lie. He didn't need to know about the panic swimming in her breast. The pull of the past heaving on her mind.

He sighed. "Me too."

His footsteps thudded in time to hers on the path behind her. Soothing. Frightening. "Where are you from, Simon?"

"Bristol originally. We moved to Knoxville when I was in middle school. Been here ever since. You?"

"Lived in Sharps Chapel growing up. Knoxville now. What are your skill sets?"

"You get right to the point, don't you?"

"Never seen any sense in beating around the bush. You'll figure out I'm pretty direct, I suppose." And he could like it or not. As long as he finished the challenge. The more space she forced between them the better.

"I am a proficient bow hunter. Decent shelter builder. Patient listener."

Good. She had skills with a small knife, but the machete she brought wouldn't be a throwing-to-kill kind of weapon. "Glad you brought the bow and arrows. Should be helpful. I hope you can use them as well as you say."

He chuckled. "Me too."

Humble too, apparently. This was going to be an

interesting thirty days.

She had to have Cherokee blood somewhere in her family line. Gorgeous. And those eyes. They drew Simon in, though he could tell she guarded them with care. She was brusque, but he didn't mind too much. As long as she held up her end of the bargain and stayed until the challenge was over, he could deal with the straightforwardness. He'd been doing that for years anyway. People never hesitated to tell him how they felt about his past conviction. Strange how being an ex-convict seemed to give people the idea they could say whatever they wanted to him and not hurt his feelings.

Three men with cameras trotted along behind him, silently filming their movements and conversation. He hadn't ever been on camera before that he knew. It was weird to think people would be watching him on their televisions. What would they think of him? If he was lucky, the jail issue wouldn't come up.

The forest teemed with life. Chipmunks darting. Squirrels barking. Birds chirping. That was a good sign. They'd have food out here.

"Hey, Fern, what's your favorite game animal to eat?"

She tilted her head to the left for a moment and then straightened it.

Cute. Did she know she did that?

"I'd say squirrel."

"Not venison?"

"I do love venison, but squirrel has this nutty flavor I love. Especially in dumplings."

"Hmm, I guess that's true. Maybe from their diet?"

"I assume so."

She didn't get his joke. He smiled. All right. New tactic. "What do you do for a living?"

"Veterinarian."

Whoa. She was smart too. Smarter than him. More successful. Why was she out here? "We still headed the correct direction?"

"Yes."

Her curt reply needled him. She didn't look down at the compass. Or tilt her head. She liked to be in charge. Fine with him.

Fern stopped and pointed to the right. "Pink flags start here."

A curving line fanned out from either side of their path and disappeared into the vast brown and green. What waited beyond those flags that made Gregory so touchy about staying within them? He gave them one more glance and then refocused his efforts on keeping up with Fern's quick pace. Even with his long legs, he had no doubt she could outdistance him on pure determination alone. "Must be in the right place. He said they flagged off a hundred-acre section, right?"

"Yes. We need to find water."

Duh. Sweat dripped off his forehead every time he looked at the ground. Plastered his pack to his back. "I agree."

"The three most important things out here. Water, shelter, food. In that order."

Did she think him a simpleton? He bit his cheek and held in a snarky reply.

"Come on. We want to find a place to set up camp before dark."

He risked a glance at the cameraman directly behind him. The man raised his eyebrows as if to say, "Wow." Simon smiled. His thought exactly. It was going to be a long month with this beautiful, no-nonsense woman.

Cicadas buzzed somewhere over Fern's head, hidden among the leaves. Singing in waves, first left, then right. Calm, then blaring. Like a buggy chorus pulsing words unintelligible to human ears. As the sun rose, the humidity skyrocketed. Fern's shirt and pants clung to her, rubbing between her thighs, under her arms. Breathing became harder as they continued on an overall downward slope, zigzagging across its face. "We need water." Her throat didn't want to release the words, wanted to hold them fast like one of those sticky traps for mice or bugs laid vertical in her throat. She attempted to produce some spit to swallow. It was getting more difficult with each step. The water bottles on the cameramen's belts were torturing her. The sound of the sloshes amplified in her dry ears.

She'd only been hiking a few short hours. How could she be so thirsty already? More importantly, was Simon in the same state as she?

"Yep, getting pretty thirsty here."

Good. Same as her. He wouldn't think her weak for needing a drink. She peered back at the mountain they'd descended. Surely they must be nearing the base. And, if they were lucky, there would be a valley and a source of water. They just had to find it. She'd made sure to eat a breakfast packed full of protein, and so far it had worked to stave off any sense of hunger. How much longer would that last though? She was burning calories fast, and the work was only beginning. Once they found a suitable campsite, they would need to erect a shelter. More like two. She had no plans to share the same sleeping quarters with Simon.

She'd also checked the weather forecast before she left. No chance of rain today or tomorrow. But the third day was supposed to be stormy. They needed to fortify their shelters before then. Yes, a lot of work faced them. Would they have time to find a food source too? Even slugs and bugs would work. She glanced around, again taking in the surroundings. There was no shortage of fallen and rotting trees, which was a good sign for grub and fungus life. She had never eaten a grub. The mere thought rather turned her stomach, but this was survival at its core. She didn't have room to be picky. Maybe if they put them in a soup with some mushrooms, it would be somewhat edible.

"Fern, look out!"

She jumped and froze, left foot balancing precariously on the edge of a vertical drop of more than twenty-five feet. Her jaw muscles tensed to the point they ached. Strong hands gripped her shoulders, gently urging her backward. How had she been so lost in thought she'd walked blindly? "Er . . . Thanks."

"That was a close one. You okay?" His crease-lined hazel eyes searched hers. "What were you thinking about?"

She shook her head. "Nothing. Let's keep moving."

Ducking away from his concern, she attempted to pick a path along the top of the rim. They had to find a way down. She was such an idiot, nearly stepping off a cliff and needing Simon to save her. Her insides crawled. She didn't make stupid mistakes like this. What was wrong with her? She peered around at the cameras. Her rookie mistake would no doubt be one of the clips Gregory decided to air. Ugh. She'd look like a moron in front of everyone in the whole United States.

She straightened her shoulders. No more mistakes.

The terrain in front of them sloped down sharply, circling around to the base of the cliff. They rounded a corner, and she paused to listen. The musical tinkle of trickling water surrounded them. She licked her lips.

"Look." Simon tapped her elbow.

She followed the length of his outstretched arm. A beautiful ribbon of clear water poured over the precipice on the far end. Splashed into a rocky pool and trailed out in a wide creek. Fern sighed. For the next month, this was home.

Simon spun in a slow circle, taking in the setting and resources. Lots of shady cover. Good. Steady flow of water. Good. He strode to the rock and touched its cool, vertical face. Mostly rock. A smidgen of mud tucked in the creases. Barely enough for plants to grow, but small trees, ferns, and grasses clung to the sides. The creek babbled lightly, clear and fresh. There should be no reason for it to dry up completely. Good.

Fern had scared him up top. He had no clue what she had been thinking, but it had consumed her to the point she'd almost fallen to her death. He'd have to keep his eye on her. Maybe she wasn't as self-sufficient as she'd like others to believe.

"This place is perfect. Wish we could get a drink now."

"Need to boil it first." She turned and began to walk away from him. "Come on, we've got a lot of work to do."

If he had hackle feathers, they would be rising.

Did she not hear the tone in her own voice? She didn't even know about his past yet, and she already treated him like he was beneath her. He snorted and strode in the opposite direction. One cameraman followed him, the other trailed after Fern. He didn't care what the third did. If she didn't have the fire starter in her pack, he would've gotten to work building one. He was parched, but he needed some space before he said something he would regret. He did have to be alone with this woman for a long time. If he could help it, neither of them would be giving up either. The prize money was worth her chilly tone. The fresh start it would provide worth her ice darts.

He approached the creek and knelt. Dipped his hands in the water and rubbed them over his sticky face and neck. How he longed to take a drink! It wouldn't do to be sick on the first day though. Too many possibilities for parasites and bacteria. He had no clue how many animals visited this water source, but hopefully a lot. If he and Fern minimized their impact, maybe they could avoid scaring all the wildlife away right off. Mosquitoes hovered over the water in the shadier places. Water striders slid silently across the surface. A flash of silver scales below the surface made his heart skip. There were fish here. A great sign.

"We need to get busy."

Fern's voice right behind him made him jump.

"You're not drinking that are you?"

He took a deep breath through flared nostrils and counted to ten. Flashed a smile with his calm reply.

"Wouldn't dream of it." Boss, he wanted to add but bit his tongue.

"Good. I picked out a site for my shelter."

Her shelter? Seriously? His jaw dropped.

"You can build yours nearby. As soon as we finish mine, I'll cut wood and help you fix yours too."

"We're building two shelters?" That made no sense whatsoever. More labor. Less body heat on cold nights.

"You expected me to cuddle?"

No. Who would want to cuddle with a hedgehog? How could he respond without heat lacing his words? He bit his tongue again. It would be sore before the day was over. "Lead the way."

Fern led him to a grassy clearing surrounded by tall tulip poplars not fifty feet from the creek. A pile of long, straight branches already awaited them.

"You've been a busy beaver."

She shrugged. "Idle hands, you know."

Was that directed at him? "I don't think we should camp so close to the creek. There are a ton of mosquitoes."

"Do we really want to have to hike to our water source?"

He was going to lose his carefully guarded patience. Soon. "I'd rather hike than be eaten alive. Besides, we don't want to scare the prey animals away from the water. We can camp a little farther away and save ourselves a lot of headache."

Fern hacked another branch off the nearest tree

with one swipe of her machete. "Fine. I'll camp here. You choose your own spot."

His eyebrows knitted together so tightly his forehead felt as if it would cramp. Two separate camps? Not to mention if she stayed here, she'd still be scaring the animals away. And they'd both be alone. Better to stay here and keep watch in case she started to do anything foolish again. He gritted his teeth. Exhaled. "Fine. Want me to start cutting?"

She spun on him so fast, he took a step back.

"You think I can't cut the limbs because I'm a woman?"

Whoa. Where did that come from? He was trying to be nice and she was liable to whip his head off with the next stroke. He raised both hands. "Not at all. Trying to be helpful."

"I don't need your help. Thank you."

"I'll gather firewood." Anything to distance himself from her uncalled-for rage. And the cute way she lifted her shoulders and tossed her ponytail over her shoulder when she was giving him instructions. Good grief. Cute? She was spiny and cold and bossy. None of those things were in the same county as cute. What was wrong with him? Dehydrated? Hungry? Both. His brain wasn't firing on all cylinders. That's all it was. Thirty days with Dr. Fern Strongbow may prove harder than he'd anticipated.

He spun away from her and marched back toward the creek, pausing to watch the cameramen work. Once they realized the juicy argument was over, they set the cameras on tripods and began rigging the smaller, motion-activated ones all around the camp and creek. How they fit so many in their packs, Simon couldn't be sure. When they finished, the forest had at least a hundred photographic eyes ready to record their every move. One more reason for him to keep his cool at all costs. It wouldn't help him persuade the audience of his value if he lost his temper on camera.

Simon grabbed his Go-Pro from his backpack, slipped it over his head, and plunged into the dense forest south of their camp. He followed the creek as best he could over downed trees and around briar patches, picking up manageable sticks and portions of logs he could break free with his hands. Soon he had an armful and turned his mind back toward camp and Fern's prickly attitude. How would they work together for an entire month?

Maybe she was nervous about the challenge. He was, too, but he was more nervous now about being partners. His brain split down the middle. Literally and figuratively. He chuckled at his own pun. One half wanted to throw up walls the height of the Empire State Building. Shut her out and survive this thing alone. The other wanted to rush to her side and watch the way she moved. Her talent and love for this type of thing evident in the deft movements of her slender hands.

Crackling leaves ahead made him stop in his tracks. He breathed quietly in and out, forcing his heart rate to slow. A trim, tan form emerged from the blackberry vines not twenty paces away. The doe munched on blackberries, picking them one by one from the bush with careful lips. Why hadn't he grabbed his bow?

Fern paused to wipe sweat from her brow. What was taking Simon so long? She peered around the grove, especially noting the darker shady places. There was no movement.

She had bitten his head off when he offered help. Hadn't meant to, but he'd taken it well. He'd get over it. She'd have to make an effort to be a bit softer.

Had he fallen? Gotten lost? Though birds chirped overhead, the sudden emptiness of their camp swallowed her. If only Simon would hurry back, she wouldn't be alone. She may not be comfortable with him, but he afforded a sense of protection she hadn't expected. There was safety in numbers. In another set of eyes to watch for trouble. Not to mention how pleasant he was to look at. Whoa. She needed to stop that thought right in its tracks. He was her partner. That was it. Like a business arrangement. Once the show was over and they had their money, they'd go their separate ways and she'd never have to see him again.

"Hello there!"

Fern smiled. She was relieved he'd returned? Happy even? Interesting. "Over here."

He appeared with a dirt-streaked face.

She took a deep breath. "How'd that go?"

"Got some to get us started. Looks like you've made good progress."

Though she didn't want to, her heart had a mind of its own. It gave a pleasant flutter with his compliment. "Working my tail off while you were gallivanting around this beautiful forest." She meant it as a joke, a way to ease the tension she'd inadvertently created between them. But, his grimace told her she'd used the wrong tone of voice. Again. Why couldn't she ever get stuff like that right?

"I was kidding."

He squeezed his lips together and nodded. "Can I use the fire starter?"

"Oh, I'll get it. I could use a break anyway."

Simon's shoulders slumped.

She mustered up a pleasant tone. "Why don't you look for some cordage so we can start assembling the shelters?" She glanced at the sky. "We are burning through the hours fast today."

"Sure thing." He spun on his heels and disappeared again.

Why couldn't she have given him the fire starter? Did she always have to be in control of everything?

Yes. Yes, she did.

Simon may hate it, but she was good at being in charge. Things happened effectively, efficiently when she directed them. He would thank her later when things got tougher and she kept her cool. Besides, she'd be less stressed if she was in charge. Less worried about Simon being attracted to her if she acted ugly. She could master whatever these crazy butterflies in her tummy were whenever he was near. Squash them flat and stomp on them until they couldn't rise again.

With her machete, she peeled away bark and scraped some tinder from one of the branches Simon had found. Built a tepee of twigs around the tinder and pulled the fire starter from her pack. With the first strike of the Ferro-rod against the steel, sparks burst out. But the wood shavings didn't catch. Again, she struck the steel. Nothing. Again and again she created sparks, but the tinder refused to ignite.

She'd done this a million times. Why wasn't it lighting? Too wet, perhaps. She gripped the rod tighter. Pressed her lips together. Come on. Thirst clawed at the back of her throat. They had to have fire. Had to have a drink before dehydration took them out of the contest on the first day.

Simon's footsteps approached behind. He leaned over her shoulder. Watched as she made a fool of herself once more.

With a low growl, she flung the fire starter to the ground. "This is impossible. Too wet."

"May I give it a go?"

"Help yourself. I doubt it will work though."

The gentle smirk on his face drove nails into her chest. He'd see. If she couldn't make a fire with wet tinder, why did he think he would succeed?

She popped to her feet and sudden dizziness fringed the edges of her vision with black. Doubling over, she placed both hands on her knees and took a few deep breaths. Dehydration was no joke.

Simon was in the process of disassembling her tepee. He laid the sticks in a neat pile and formed a nest-like shell of the tinder. Then, gently, he struck the rod. The sparks caught in the shavings bowl and a tiny tendril of smoke curled upward.

Okay, fine. He could do better than she. Good for him. It had been years since she had to do this type of thing. The rust would fall away from her skills soon.

Simon lifted the tinder nest to his lips and blew in slow puffs until a flame leapt from the shavings. A shiver crept up her spine. Her gaze, glued to the tender way he blew on the flames, refused to obey her commands to look at something else. Anything else.

He set the ball of fire on the bare ground she'd cleared and laid the twigs in a perfect tepee over the flames.

"Good job." She gave him a weary smile.

"Thanks."

"Give me your pot and I'll fetch some water."

He shoved the large kettle into her outstretched hand. She made her way to the creek and dipped the pot in the cool water. The thought of a long drink made her mouth even drier. Already the stream lay in shade as the sun hid behind the trees framing their horizon. They'd be sleeping under the stars tonight. If only the predicted thunderstorms would skirt around them.

Tomorrow would be easier. A dark cloud cruised over the opening in the canopy and parked directly overhead. Thoughts of sleeping next to Simon by the quiet orange glow gave rise to trembling hands. How would she ever make it through this challenge? Why wouldn't her heart and body listen to her arguments to stop fawning like a naïve, young girl? Didn't she know better?

Simon pressed the little, round button and smiled into the lens. "This is diary cam number one. Um, I don't know if I need to number them. But," he snickered. "This is a bit awkward, isn't it? Okay, let me start over."

He ran a hand over his beard and cleared his throat. "Diary entry number one on day one. Fern and I have started to set up camp. We've found a good, clean water source and have a fire going." He turned the camera to show the fire. "She's gone to fetch water now, and soon we won't be thirsty anymore!" That was a bit too enthusiastic. He should tone it down a bit so he didn't sound like such an idiot. "Things are going okay between us. Fern is a bit prickly, but she's going to be a great partner." He shouldn't have said that. This was harder than it looked. "Well, good night. Hopefully tomorrow we will get a shelter finished." He switched off the camera and tucked it back inside its waterproof bag.

A shelter. One out of two. He really should argue with her more and try to get his point across. But was it worth it?

Chapter 6

Evening settled in gradations of grey. Black and white, an old movie. Daytime sounds ceased, giving a brief lull in the noise. Fern blinked, it seemed, and darkness was as solid as a wall outside the perimeter of the bouncing orange firelight. Chirrups and peeps exploded in a cacophonous song. The breeze ceased to rustle the leaves and cool her neck, and with its absence, a swarm of mosquitoes rose and attacked them. Fern slapped a few on her forearms, but soon their pinching, itchy bites penetrated her shirt. The whine of their wings became the most audible sound in her periphery.

"This is insane! Where do they all come from?"

Simon didn't reply. He seemed too busy swatting at them himself.

Already her back itched in a hundred places. Her cheeks, covered in bumps. Her scalp, alive with the tickle of their feet in her hair. She couldn't stand this. Not for a month of nights. Not for this night. "We have to move, Simon."

"How exactly do you plan to accomplish that in the dark?"

Panic rose steadily higher in her throat. It didn't matter how, she had to get away from the incessant whir near her ears, their piercing mouths digging into her flesh.

Fern sprang to her feet and grabbed a long stick. She plunged it into the fire until the bark on its tip ignited. "Come on."

At first, she didn't register whether his footsteps followed or not. Nothing but the ringing buzz of the tortuous little bugs sounded in her ears. An impenetrable cloud of the demons hovered around her head, following her mercilessly into the black forest.

"Fern, slow down. You can't run away from them."

Simon's strong hand gripped her shoulder. It seemed to have a home there now, no longer startling. Rather comforting. She paused her retreat.

"Let's go back to the fire and use the ash to coat our skin. It will help."

"I can't. They're driving me crazy." She rubbed her hand across each ear in turn. "The sound of them is piercing my brain."

"Okay, we can help that too. We will find some dry leaves and use them like cotton balls."

That made more sense than diving into the

woods. Why hadn't she thought of it? Some of the fierce tension ebbed away as he held out his hand for hers.

"Come on."

"Okay." How was he so calm? Were the mosquitoes not bugging him too? And why were they bugging her so much? Where had the Fern she thought she knew gone? She took a deep breath and allowed him to take her hand. He led her back to their fire, where he grabbed a bit of ash from the perimeter and turned to her.

"Here."

He rubbed her face with warm ash, stirring those jittery feelings in her stomach. The gentleness of his hands surprised her. She wanted to shrink from his fingers. Yet, she wanted to linger under their sweet touch forever. He finished her face and hovered over her neckline. Her eyes grew wider.

He cleared his throat. "Here, you finish up." He dumped a handful of ash into her open palm and turned back to the fire.

She coated her neck, front and back, and her arms. Too bad she couldn't reach her back, but that was territory she definitely wouldn't allow Simon's help. His simple touch on her face had caused enough molten lava to ignite in her abdomen. She was liable to catch fire if he touched her back.

Once the gritty ash coated her, the mosquito bites slacked, but the droning sound of their wings still reminded her of the nightmare she had in times of stress. An alarm clock on her nightstand would ring mercilessly, endlessly, even though she pushed the button to stop the blaring. Even though she unplugged it. Smashed it to smithereens with a hammer. The beep, beep, beep would continue. Drilling into her mind. Nearly deafening her until she felt she was mad with rage and fear.

"Here. These are lamb's ear leaves. They're nice and soft."

Fern stared at the familiar, furry leaves rolled between Simon's fingers. When she made no move to help or reply, he lifted the strands of stray hair and gently wiggled the leaves into her ear canals. Not far. Just enough to block out the sounds of torture.

He smiled and returned to his place beside the fire.

She opened her mouth. Closed it again. Sighed and took a deep breath. "Thank you. For that."

"You're welcome."

Frowning, she cupped a hand to her ear. "What? I can't hear you."

"Ha. Ha. Very funny."

A giggle, both nervous and relieved, escaped her. "I mean it. You've been . . . my hero today." Had she really said that aloud?

He nodded and patted the ground next to him. "We need to try to sleep."

Sleep would feel wonderful. Her muscles cried for rest, her feet burned, and her skin itched. She gave in and sank to the ground. Not exactly where he patted, but a little bit closer than before.

Simon stretched out and closed his eyes. How strange to be so exposed, so vulnerable. The last time he hunted at least he had a tent surrounding him at night. Even though the thin canvas probably afforded little actual protection from bear claws and massive storms, it had made him feel safer. The fire protected them from one small area, but what about the rest of the forest? Anything could creep in while they slept.

If they slept. The ground didn't exactly invite it. Nor the hoard of insects. Or Fern's tossing and swatting. Exhaustion lay so deep in his body, he was past the point of easy slumber. His eyes popped open.

The stars didn't exist in the cloud-filled sky beyond the treetops. Not a good sign. Why had he not insisted on a camp farther from the water? He'd wanted to avoid an argument on the first day, sure, but it was more than that, wasn't it? He wanted Fern to like him. If only he could keep her from finding out about his stint in prison, maybe he could gain her trust in the next few days. Then when she found out, they would be friends, and it would be harder for her to scorn him.

Ha. Some plan. His friends from high school had abandoned him like he was the shark and they were the seals sprinting for shore. None of them were left when he was released. Not one. Why should he hope Fern would be any different? The one difference was she was stuck with him, good or bad, rain or shine, until they saw this thing through.

He dug a rock from under his back and tossed it into the trees. Shifted so he faced the darkness. Fern's rhythmic breathing told him she'd managed to drift off. Good. He wanted her to have a peaceful night's rest. Maybe tomorrow she'd be less standoffish.

She was lying not more than a couple feet from him. Her warm, curvy body and long, dark hair only a few inches away. All he would have to do is move, just a little, and he'd feel the rhythm of her pulse against his. Move just a little and feel the gentle rhythm of her breath through those luscious lips.

Don't be an idiot. Simon crossed his arms over his chest and scooted farther from her.

His eyes slid closed as a cool breeze drifted into camp. He needed sleep. Come on, brain, turn off already. Come on hormones, go back to hibernation.

A rustle in the leaves nearby made his eyelids fly open once more. He sat up, taking care not to make noise. It was good Fern was resting. Her near-miss earlier and her near-freak out a bit ago were worrisome. On the outside she appeared to be strong, confident. But underneath she had issues.

Like him. Could they bond over that? He had to admit he rather liked taking care of her. Protecting her. Playing the hero.

But he was no hero. Far from it. How long would it be until she realized?

A stick popped in the shadows. Simon whipped his head around. Something was there. Potential food? Or potential predator?

Soft footsteps crunched in the fallen leaves, closer. Heavy-sounding. If only he had a flashlight. His hand crept to the bow near his feet. He gripped an arrow and slid it into the notch. Took a deep breath. Let it out slowly.

The steps grew nearer. A few more feet and he would bet he could get a visual. He'd be ready to snag a meal. And protect sleeping Fern. She may grow to hate him soon, but for now he would watch over her like the noble sentinel he wished he was.

A low sound like a throaty growl rumbled from the forest. Magnified in his keenly piqued ears. He raised the bow. Drew the string taut. Waited. Breath frozen in his chest.

The animal's dark form appeared like a faint mist through the trees less than ten feet from them. Shorter than he expected. A bobcat? A boar? His fingers trembled. Come on beast, a few more steps.

The animal paused, still too shadowed to identify. Simon flared his nostrils and forced himself to exhale without sound.

One step. Two.

A raccoon? He sighed and almost laughed. Not a big, scary predator at all. But, still, it could be dinner.

The arrow hissed through the empty night, grazed the gray fur on the raccoon's back, and sailed into the trees.

The raccoon leapt to the side and tore away through the forest.

Drat. Necessary protein skittered away into oblivion.

He laid the bow down and pushed to his feet. Hoping not to disturb Fern, who seemed almost comatose, he dug into his pack and retrieved his journaling camera. He switched it to night vision mode and aimed it at the tree. No blood. No fur. No sign of the fat, delicious raccoon. Boy, he must be hungry.

Where was his arrow? He scanned the low vegetation, but it would have to wait till morning.

A rustle in the ferns caught his attention. What in the world?

Kneeling, he peered under a large frond. Two tiny eyes glowed green on his screen.

Apparently, the coon was a momma. What were the chances she'd come back for her little one? What were the chances it would die alone before dawn?

He gingerly scooped it up and wrapped it into the tail of his shirt.

It squealed and bared its pointy teeth.

"You're a naughty little fellow, aren't you?" Course, who could blame the little tyke? Simon had tried to kill his mother. "I'm going to take you back to camp for the night. Maybe your mommy will come back."

Too tiny to fight long, the kit went limp beneath Simon's stroke. Its trembling stopped and its eyes drifted closed.

Fern would have a surprise when she woke. Would she love it? Or hate him for his actions? He didn't know her well enough to begin to predict how she would react. But he'd like to. Maybe underneath her icy exterior there was someone soft and warm. He chuckled. Or maybe there were fangs and more sharp words.

A strange sound woke Fern. A whimper? More like a tiny whine. The veterinarian in her snapped to life. Some tiny animal needed her help. She forced her sticky, heavy eyelids open and squinted them against the blaring sun. How late was it? Where was she?

Simon. The forest. The challenge.

Right. Shielding her eyes with her arm, she peeled them open again and glanced around. Simon was nowhere to be seen, but a fire in the ring of rocks they'd placed yesterday hissed as water splashed over the top of the pot. His button-up flannel shirt lay nearby, squirming in the middle. What in the world? Rising onto all fours, she crawled to the shirt and gently peeled back a corner. Her heart melted. A tiny raccoon kit nuzzled the flannel and squeaked.

"Oh, poor baby. You must be starving." She scooped it into her arms and cradled it to the crook of her neck. It didn't try to resist. "We will have to feed you something, won't we? Where is your momma?"

Simon stepped from the forest with an armload

of firewood and grinned. "I see you found our new friend."

"Where did he come from?"

He lowered his gaze. "I almost shot his mother last night."

It was evident by his downturned mouth he thought she'd be angry with him. But it was quite the opposite. It was impressive that he'd already tried to secure a meal. "We need to feed him."

Simon grinned.

She must've gotten her tone right for once.

He spread his arms wide and bowed. "He's all yours. Consider it a Survival Tennessee gift from me to you welcoming you to our humble abode."

She giggled. "Well, thank you, kind sir." She snuggled the little guy closer. What would she feed him? There was no way to replicate his mother's life-giving milk. Earthworm soup would have to do. Who knew? Maybe she and Simon could have some too. Her stomach turned, but she would tamp down her gut reaction. Nutrition was nutrition.

After rewrapping the kit in Simon's shirt, she grabbed her machete and headed for a rotten log she'd noticed near the creek. A wave of dizziness washed over her, fringing her periphery in black. She needed to sit down and drink water all day until her blood regained its equilibrium. The clouds had blown away sometime during the night, at least. They should have clear weather to finish their shelter-building.

Once the blackness faded, Fern snuck her fingers

under the edge of the log and rolled it toward her shins. She'd learned that rule from her dad when she was a child. Always give any snake potentially hiding underneath an escape path away from yourself. It was an easy lesson to remember after a copperhead curled under one log had shimmied away right between her flip-flopped feet when she was nine.

Fat, brown worms wiggled atop the damp earth, trying to pierce the soil and disappear again. She scooped a dozen into her open palm and carried them back to camp. Before they could slip through her fingers, she plopped them into the already boiling water. Tossed in a few plantain leaves and grabbed a stick to stir it all up. It didn't exactly make her mouth water.

Simon raised both eyebrows as Fern dumped the worms into the pot. Did she mean for them to eat the woodsy stew? If only he'd gotten the raccoon last night. No way was he putting earthworm in his mouth. It didn't matter how hungry he felt.

Her reaction to the raccoon kit stirred him. She hadn't been angry after all. In fact, she seemed very pleased with his unintentional gift. Maybe there was a soft spot in there. She was a veterinarian. Surely that meant she cared about God's creatures, and maybe even he could be included on that list.

The smells drifting from the boiling water

reminded him of the earth after a rainstorm. He risked peeking over the rim at her concoction. The fat worms lay on the bottom of the pan while the leaves floated around in circles on top. "How do you know when it's done?"

"When they stop wriggling, I guess."

Was she teasing him? "Breakfast for the raccoon?" Please. Not for them.

"And us."

His stomach constricted. She'd done something nice for them, how could he refuse? "I see."

"You're not happy with my cooking? Fine. Don't have any."

There it was. The icy bristle. "I've never eaten an earthworm before. You?"

"They're delicious. Just don't chew too much."

Now she was kidding. She had to be. "Okay. If you try it first."

She tried to stifle a snicker behind her hand. She was. She was pulling his leg. He smiled. "You're messing with me, aren't you?"

"Who? Me?"

So, Dr. Strongbow did have a humorous side. The smile she flashed his direction nearly knocked him on his backside. "I'm going to have to remember that."

"What?"

"Teasing me makes you smile."

A lovely shade of red crept onto her cheeks further highlighting her elegant cheekbones. Simon couldn't help but stare a bit longer than necessary. She turned her head and began mashing the "stew" with her stirring stick. "Do you have a scrap of fabric or something I can use to feed Dexter?"

"Dexter?" He chuckled. "Didn't take long for you to name him, did it?"

"He looks like a Dexter." She held the tiny kit up and scratched his chin. "Don't you think?"

He'd agree with Fern about anything right now, her contentment was so intoxicating. "One hundred percent." He tore a piece of the hem off his flannel shirt and handed it to her.

With the piece he handed her dripping with earthworm soup, she gingerly placed it against Dexter's mouth and waited for him to begin sucking. "See, he likes it. Must be pretty tasty, eh?"

Oh, yeah right. He nodded.

They sat in silence filled only by Dexter's contented purrs until the little guy had his fill and began licking his front paws.

"You're up, Dad."

Dad? He knit his eyebrows together. Fern seemed to realize what she'd said and the blush he'd seen earlier didn't begin to compare to the one that blossomed on her cheeks now. It took all his reserve to tamp down a chuckle.

"Sorry. That came out weird. I only meant because you found him and all. And . . ."

His thoughts were zooming to places they shouldn't be heading. He cleared his throat. "No worries. Ladies first. I insist."

Fern placed Dexter in her lap and took the pot. Brought it to her lips and mumbled from behind the metal, "Here goes nothing."

Simon frowned at the sound of her first slurp, fully expecting her to spew the soup onto the ground. When she drank deeply, and then wiped the back of her hand across her mouth, he swallowed hard. "Well?"

"Swallow without chewing. If you do it fast, you can't taste a thing." She smirked and handed him the pot.

The look on her face was a challenge. No question about it. She was testing his pride. His very manhood. He'd show her. With one quick look into the pot, he raised it to his lips and slugged as much as he could stand. Though bitterness crept into his throat after he swallowed, he refused to let her see it on his face. "Tasty." His stomach turned. Fern's giggles followed him into the forest as he raced away to find a quiet place to be sick.

Chapter 7

Fern felt badly for Simon. Really, she did. She didn't mean to laugh at his discomfort. Nuzzling Dexter's chin with her forefinger, she waited for Simon to return when a strange sound reached her. She glanced at the sky as a white drone soared over the tree line into the opening above their camp. "What in the world?"

The drone lowered like a slow-motion hummingbird. Something hanging from its plastic runners waved in the breeze caused by the four little propellers. Once it was close enough, Fern retrieved the drone's cargo and opened the envelope. The drone rose and disappeared into the sky.

DARE

You have four hours to build your shelter. In that time, you can ponder your first clue:

Lost at sea

In the middle of the trees?
This coveted item will change your nights.
Simon must dive.

Remember, you must complete each one in order to receive the next. The faster you figure them out, the quicker the game will go. The quicker you will get to go home richer individuals. Ready. Set. Go.

She shook the envelope again. A timer fell into her palm. "Three hours and forty-five minutes left?" That wasn't enough time to erect a passable shelter. Let alone two. "Simon!"

He emerged from the forest with a pale face.

"You have earthworm in your beard." She suppressed another giggle as he swiped his shaking hand over his lips.

"We need real meat."

She waved the paper. "No time for that. We have a clue. And a timer."

He plopped onto the ground beside her and read the note. If it were possible, his skin grew paler. "Dive?"

"That's what it says."

"Got any idea what it means?"

"So far, we've only seen one source of water." She motioned with her thumb toward their watering hole. "I don't think it's deep enough to dive, do you?"

"Dunno. Clear as the water is, it's hard to judge how deep it is."

"Well, apparently we aren't to go there until this timer beeps. That gives us," she checked the time again, "Three hours and forty minutes to build some sort of shelter."

"Mr. Vanderbilt said this would be a hard challenge. He wasn't kidding, was he?"

"Better put your big boy boots on today. Come on. You find cordage." She didn't wait to see his reaction. They had work to do. And lots of it.

Fern marched into the forest with her machete held before her. She chopped an armful of long sticks and carried them back to camp. Simon was again absent. Hopefully, he was doing what she'd told him to.

After her fourth trip, Simon reappeared in camp and dumped a load of grapevine and honeysuckle at her feet. "You know, this would've been a lot easier with the knife."

His tone, edged in thorns, bristled. Her shoulder muscles tensed. "We can't both have it. It's my survival tool."

"Fine. Have it your way, your highness." He bowed in the same fashion as when she'd discovered Dexter. But this time when he rose, he spun and stomped away.

It was obvious she had upset him. But he didn't understand. She needed the machete. At all times. It was the only thing protecting her from him. And the memories.

➤➤➤ ➤

Fern was the most infuriating, belittling, patronizing woman he'd ever met. Selfish. Arrogant. Beautiful. The last one stopped him in his retreat. Good grief. She'd made his blood boil and he was still noticing the way her eyes reflected the summer sun in a rich, ebony light. The way her black hair glistened when rays piercing their forest canopy touched the top of her head. Why, why, why was she so ridiculously, completely stubborn?

He took a deep breath. Blew it out. He sure could use some of those prayers Thomas had promised. *Why don't you pray yourself?* The thought came to him on the whisper of the next breeze. It had been eons since he'd prayed. Since he'd laid his heart open for Him. Now was not the time.

"Simon!"

Oh, great. She was beckoning him. Again. Two days and it felt like Fern was his boss instead of his partner. And what was this first clue? How was he going to dive anywhere in the dense forest surrounding him? His blood pressure was rising again, tightening the muscles running up his neck. He couldn't hide from her. Or from the first challenge. Unless he went home . . . No. He wasn't a quitter. Never had been. Wouldn't start now. He'd been playing the part of ex-con for years now and no one was any the wiser. If he could force himself to hold onto the secret that had changed his life, he could force himself to stay. Even with the most frustrating person he'd been made to spend time with. Ever.

"I'm coming!" He yanked a few more honeysuckle vines free from the bank they clung to and wound them around his arm and shoulder like an electrical cord. His palms and finger creases burned from pulling the plants free. They were as tough as baling twine. It took every ounce of reserve not to mumble complaints with each step on his return.

Fern had a makeshift lean-to erected at the base of an oak tree, with one long stick protruding horizontally supported by others stretching to the ground at obtuse angles. She held the end of the horizontal limb up with her shoulder as she stretched to grab another stick from her pile. Yep, stubborn.

"Let me help you." He dropped the vines and took the weight of the shelter in his hands.

"Thanks. Heavier than I thought."

Her tone had softened considerably, as had the lines around her mouth. She looked almost content at her task.

"Hand me a vine, will you? I'll get busy tying this end up and you can work on the other." He was taking a gamble with his life attempting to direct her.

She inhaled, cocked her head, and shrugged. "Sounds good."

He still had his head on his shoulders. Surprising. Maybe God was watching over their situation even though he didn't have the courage to pray. They worked in tandem without speaking for a long while. Simon was thankful for the silence. It gave him time to realign his thoughts.

Dexter began whining as they tied the last honeysuckle vine.

"Oh, please, Fern. No more earthworm soup."

She scooped Dexter into her arms and smiled. "I don't know what you're complaining about. We thought it was delicious. Didn't we, Dexter?"

The timer beeped. Fern moved to silence it. "I guess it's time, eh?"

He nodded. The pool couldn't be that deep. Could it?

Fern took a long swig of their boiled water and handed him the pot. He drank as much as his stomach could hold, then dumped the rest and took Dexter from her. Slipped the baby coon into the pot and handed it back to her. "That should hold him while we figure this out."

A dark cloud drifted over the sun. The crystal clear water lost its sparkle. "Here goes nothing." Simon removed his shoes and t-shirt and waded in. The iciness bit through his pants and sent a sharp shiver through him. Good old mountain streams. Always cold. Figured. "Did I mention I'm not that great of a swimmer?"

"Ah! Even better." Gregory clapped his hands once and leaned closer to the monitor.

Turner turned to him and squinted. "Did you know Simon couldn't swim?"

"Nope. Icing on the cake, as they say."

"He could drown."

"Exactly. This should speed things up considerably."

"Speed what up, exactly? I didn't sign on for a felony here."

Gregory pressed a finger to his lips and shushed his best friend. It was perfect. This first exercise better than he had planned. Ought to be a doozy of a christening into the challenge. He chuckled watching Simon cautiously slide into the water and Fern rolling her eyes. They were getting along swimmingly so far. Needling each other and bringing out the hidden flaws Gregory hoped to uncover. Tomorrow's test would be even more revealing. And he would know if they lied. He'd whisk away their new acquisition from today if they did. They'd learn soon enough not to push the limit of his laws.

Watching through the lens wasn't nearly as fulfilling as he'd hoped. He needed to see firsthand their reactions to each other. To feel the palpable emotions in the air. Only then could he truly discern their weaknesses. Truly taste their frustrations and discover their breaking points.

Fern's eyebrows shot upward. "Let me do it. I was on the swim team."

He didn't have time to debate. His toes were

already burning from the cold water. "Remember the note? It said it had to be me."

She groaned. "Right. Well, better hurry then."

"Couldn't agree more. Be right back." He sucked in two lungfuls of air, pinched his nose, and dropped under the water. It was deeper than he'd imagined. Rotating so his feet were up and head down, he pulled with his free hand and sank down. The circumference narrowed the lower he swam. In ten feet or so he was at the bottom and surrounded by layered rocks of all different sizes. Too small. Too cramped. Too much like a prison cell. He kicked at the gravelly bottom and rocketed to the surface.

"See anything?"

"No," he spluttered.

"There's got to be something. Want me to try?"

Did he ever. "No. Rules." How was he going to get past the panic rising in his chest long enough to do a search of any kind? A strong wind riffled through the trees, showing their silver undersides.

Fern whipped her gaze upward. "Better hurry, Simon. Really. It looks like rain."

No pressure at all. With another deep breath and shiver, he aimed for the pool's floor. Without the brilliant light of the sun, the crevices contained nothing but shadows. He swallowed. Pressed down the need for a breath. And closed his eyes. The space around him was not shrinking. It wasn't closing in. Focus. He snapped his eyelids wide and let a bit of air escape. He searched under what seemed like a rock ledge with both hands. Rocks. Sand. There. Far to the back of the little opening sat something wooden. The grain running vertical, like slats on the side of a box.

He shot to the surface, gulped in another breath, and returned before Fern could question him. His pounding heart warned him he'd needed more time to catch his breath. He pulled on the box, but it wouldn't budge. He needed a lever. Something to pry it free. His lungs burned as he cast his gaze in a circle around him. Nothing but stones and water.

Simon shot to the surface, flailed a couple times, and flopped onto the bank at Fern's feet. "Found . . ." He sucked in another breath. "Something."

She leaned into his field of vision, her hands planted on her knees. "You okay?"

"Never better." Except for his pounding heart, aching lungs, and whirling thoughts. His prison cell was bigger than the space at the bottom of the pool. And he could breathe there. "I need something to pry it loose."

Fern disappeared and came back moments later holding a sturdy branch. "This work?"

Still trying to regain his normal breathing rate, he nodded. He had to go back down there. Back into the cramped space. The drifting clouds had congealed, forming a threatening layer of dark gray overhead. He didn't want to be in the water if those clouds held lightning. He shoved his hand out and took the stick Fern offered. Plunging headfirst into the pool this time, he aimed for the cubby where the box had been tucked.

Shoved the stick into the space he could feel around the box's edges and pushed. With a grating sound magnified in his ears under the water, he felt the container shift. He plunged his left hand into the hole, slipped his fingers under the front edge, and lifted with the stick and his hand at the same moment. It shifted a second time. Sharp pain pinched his fingers, instantly turning to throbbing heat. No, no, no. He yanked. Pain shot into his wrist. *Lord?* The box refused to budge.

He was trapped in a new kind of prison.

Help! His throat strained. Air escaped in a large whoosh with his muffled scream.

Something was wrong. It was taking Simon too long this time. She'd counted the time of each of his dive attempts, and this one stretched past the prior ones. She couldn't see the front half of his body. Why weren't his feet kicking like before?

Forget the rules! The water prickled her skin as she dove in and pulled hard twice with cupped hands. Simon lay still, his hand stretched into the recesses of a black hole perpendicular to the floor. Tiny bubbles poured from his nostrils in a dancing stream toward the surface.

She yanked the stick from under his limp body and shoved it into the hole. It grated against rock. Hopefully, not his hand. But she could fix that later. He wouldn't have much use for it if he was dead.

Hooking her feet beneath the bottom rock of the ledge, she pushed with all her strength. Simon's hand floated free as the box sank to the bottom of the pool. She dropped the stick and grabbed his belt loop. He couldn't drown. Not if she could help it.

He was heavier than she would've thought. She looped both arms around his waist and shoved off the floor. When their heads broke through the surface, Fern gulped down a massive breath and lugged Simon to shore. He landed half on top of her, her back pressed into the rocky ground.

"Simon." She shook him. "Simon?" She wriggled free and rolled him onto his back. Felt his pulse. It was steady but slow. She leaned in and opened his mouth. No breath sounds. Using her index finger to raise his chin, she pinched his nose with the other hand. His cold lips, blue though they were, still sent a shiver zinging down her spine. She forced a breath into his chest, pulled back, and counted to ten. Another breath.

Simon spluttered and sucked in a breath. With a deep cough, his eyes flew open.

She rolled him onto his side. "Oh, thank goodness." Fern patted his back as he continued to cough. "You're going to be okay. Just breathe."

The gurgling cough slowly subsided. Simon rolled onto his back and looked up at her. "I am not going back in there."

She chuckled. "Fair enough." She leaned closer and pressed her lips to his ear. "We will have to break the rules. I'll go."

He shook his head.

"I'll be fine." Yanking back, she put her fingers to her lips, tingling where they'd brushed his earlobe. What was this sensation rocketing through her? She wasn't going to wait around and find out. She jumped to her feet and dove headfirst into the crystalline pool.

With Simon waiting above, the water cooled her body and her emotions. Just adrenaline. Had to be. The chest waited for her on the rocky bottom, with a letter combination padlock barring her from opening the lid. She jiggled it. Of course it didn't break free. Gregory was too well organized for that to work. How was the blasted box so heavy? No way would she be able to bring it to the surface.

Shoving to the surface, she took a much-needed breath. Simon sat on the bank where she'd left him, arms draped over his knees. "There's a lock. I need a four-letter word to open it."

His brow wrinkled. "Your name?"

She frowned. "Maybe. Lemme try."

Fern didn't work. Neither did the next five words they tried. When she surfaced the fifth time, Simon's frown had deepened.

"Seth."

"Who's Seth?"

Simon pursed his lips and chewed on his cheek. "Try it."

Her teeth chattered as she turned the dials and tugged on the lock. It popped loose. She opened the lid and peered inside. They'd done it. She grabbed ahold of the thin, green netting and swam to the surface for the final time.

Chapter 8

Fern stopped at the edge of the clearing entering their camp. Simon slammed into her, letting out a puff of breath he'd just managed to regain.

"You broke the rules."

Simon peered over Fern's head at Gregory, arms folded across his chest, frown glaring from his stiff face. He seemed so far out of place in his dark suit, it was almost enough to make Simon laugh. How had he gotten here so quickly in that get-up?

Fern's shoulders straightened under Simon's fingertips. He hadn't realized he'd grabbed her and still held after their collision. His hands dropped to his sides.

Fern marched closer to their fire pit and planted her feet wide.

He suppressed a grin at the look on her face. Gregory was in for an earful.

"You almost killed him."

Gregory shook his head. "That was an accident." He pointed an angry index finger at Simon, but never broke eye contact with Fern. "He was supposed to retrieve the item."

Fern sucked in a breath. "He tried. If I hadn't been there, he would've drowned. Besides, you put weights in the box. There wasn't a way for him to get it to the surface."

Weights? No wonder it'd felt stuck. Gregory never meant for him to succeed.

Fern slapped her fists on her hips. "Your TV show is not worth his life. Now, you can send us home if you like, but I'd do it again if I had to. Besides, he did dive. Your clue didn't say a word about me not joining him. We didn't break the rules. We stretched them. You, of all people, should appreciate that. I'm sure you've learned a lot about that in your line of work over the years."

Great. They were going home.

Gregory's face broke into a smile. "Touché, as they say, Ms. Strongbow." He tipped his funny-looking hat at her. "Do try to follow the rules to the letter from this point forward. It'd be a shame to see your half-mil headed in a different direction."

Gregory disappeared and soon they heard the sound of an ATV starting and fading into the distance.

"*Doctor* Strongbow," Fern mumbled.

Simon sat on a log next to their fire pit, laid the mosquito net behind him, and smiled at Fern. "Thanks.

For everything."

Fern broke her rock-hard stance and blushed under his gaze. "It was nothing." She turned her back to him. "I forgot Dexter. I'll be right back."

His throat burned. He coughed again. "Hurry back." But she was already gone.

With the adrenaline fading, utter exhaustion crept into every fiber. He had nothing to refuel, to replace the extreme amount of energy he'd expended. They had to find some protein. He reached for his bow standing against a nearby tree but drew his hand back. What was this tied to the end? He already knew, but after the first challenge, opening the next seemed like a really bad idea. They could call it quits. Go home. They'd be giving up the prize, but at least they would get to go home. Alive.

Fern would be disappointed in him. His hand shook as he undid the fishing twine holding the note in place. The twine he tucked in his pocket. It wasn't very long, but if he could find something to make a hook with, maybe it would prove useful.

TRUTH.

This next challenge won't be as physically demanding. But I bet it tests your resolve even more. Simon, you must tell Fern about Seth.

He groaned. Anything but that. He'd dive another hundred times to the bottom of that prison-pool. As long as he didn't have to tell her about Seth. The truth about that night. Why he'd been branded a felon. A nothing.

"Hey, I can't find Dexter."

Fern's voice floated through the trees, though he still didn't see her. He slipped the paper in his pocket and plastered a neutral look on his face. "Maybe his momma came back for him?"

She appeared at the fringe of the forest, mud smeared on her forehead and hair falling loose from her ponytail. Looking even more beautiful than when she was all put-together. His gaze lingered on her mouth. Those pale pink lips had touched his. Too bad he'd been half-dead and didn't remember it.

"I've looked everywhere."

He forced his eyes to look at hers. To focus on what she was saying. "I'm sorry. I'm sure he's fine. Come sit down and let's get that fresh water boiling." He patted the log next to him.

Fern placed the pot on the embers he'd rekindled and sank onto the opposite end of the log. "Gregory was pretty mad, huh?"

Simon chuckled. "I'd say you handled him just fine."

Her voice softened. "I don't mean to be like that, you know."

She didn't? How could her attitude be an accident? Maybe something in her past hurt her? Did successful veterinarians with gorgeous eyes and tempting lips have problems like the rest of mankind? He raised his arm to reach for her shoulder, but she shrugged away and ducked into her completed shelter. They'd worked all morning finishing it, and it was pretty decent. But he still had nowhere to sleep except out in the open. The argument from the prior day awoke in harsh whispers in his mind. Was it really only the day before? How on earth would they survive twenty-eight plus more? Would they ever truly be a team?

"Hey, come on. I'll help you look for Dexter." As much as he hated the idea of going near the water again so soon, he hated the idea of her missing the cute little guy more.

Fern peeked out of her shelter, swiped at an errant tear, and smiled. "Thanks. He's too little to be out on his own."

"Lead the way."

She followed the path they'd begun forming to the creek. It was amazing how quickly their presence had made an imprint on the virgin landscape.

Fern's soft voice cooed, "Dexter. Come here, buddy."

Simon forced himself to peek under the dense, low foliage instead of watching Fern as she moved. He'd never thought of cargo pants as flattering, till now. He mimicked Fern's actions, moving plants aside and clicking his tongue. "Come on, little fuzz ball. Where are you?"

They searched the path to the creek and along the side for a long time. There was no sign of the baby coon. As if he'd vanished. Had a hawk gotten him? A fox? He didn't want to voice his thoughts, but the longer they searched the less likely it seemed they'd find him.

Fern sank onto a nearby log and tossed tiny pebbles into the creek. "I guess he's gone."

What could he say? If he hadn't brought Dexter to her in the first place, she wouldn't be hurting now. "I'm sorry, Fern. I wish I'd never found him."

Her eyes flashed daggers his direction. "How can you say that?"

If he could crawl away like Dexter and hide right about now, he would. "I meant . . . well, you're so sad. If I hadn't found him, you wouldn't be upset."

Her features softened even as tears glistened in her eyes like glassy jewels. "It's okay."

It didn't feel like it was okay. Nothing was okay. In fact, nothing had gone the way he'd expected since the moment he'd walked into the interview.

The sun settled behind the trees amid a covering of clouds like the ribs on a washboard. Orange at their oblong fringes. Cement gray in the centers. It was going to rain. Fern shivered, though sweat trickled down her back. They'd run out of time before the storms moved in. She could smell it in the air. Feel it in the achy joint where she'd broken her toe as a teenager. It couldn't rain. Simon's shelter wasn't finished. Was she cruel enough to make him sleep without what little protection her shelter would afford? Dexter was out there somewhere potentially unprotected and starving. Had his mother truly returned for him? It was the only thought she could allow to enter her mind. Otherwise, she wouldn't be able to stop worrying about him.

"I think I'll turn in." Simon threw another log on the fire and stretched out on the bare earth. "I'm bone tired."

Fern wrapped her arms tight around her midsection. "I know what you mean. Can you believe it's only day two?"

He shook his head.

"Those earthworms are long gone. I'm starving."

Simon groaned.

She suppressed a giggle. The exertion of the day left her insides quaking. She couldn't imagine how Simon must feel. He was taller, heavier, and had nearly drowned. Tomorrow they would find something more to eat than a few leaves and some mashed up bugs.

It took Simon less time to begin snoring than it had taken him to lie down. Soft breaths escaped through his full lips. The ones she had touched against hers a few short hours ago. Cold and blue. Yet full of sparking electricity she wasn't sure she'd ever let herself dream about feeling.

She shook her head. She should be sleeping too. Not sitting with her gaze glued to his mouth. The morning would bring another day full of challenges. She hadn't done a single entry either. Gregory was already mad at her, she had better not push him. Grabbing her diary cam, she switched it to record.

"Gregory wants us to do these diaries, but we've been so busy I haven't had time. Things out here are hard. I'm sure I will adjust soon, though, and we will find food tomorrow. A lot of things I didn't expect have been coming up." Was there a way to rewind and delete that last part? It wasn't a lie. In fact, it was pure, painful truth. She was supposed to be good at this. Not feeling like the memories of her past were creeping in with the evening shadows. What had she gotten herself into? She hadn't expected life out here to be so hard. She had all the skills necessary to thrive in the wilderness. Why wasn't she performing better? Succeeding in finding more sustenance.

A rustle sounded in the undergrowth beyond the fire glow. She lifted her gaze from the camera lens and squinted. Dexter? She laid the camera beside her and slinked to her feet without a sound. Simon needed as much rest as he could get.

"Dexter?" Her whisper blared in the otherwise silent forest. Fern stopped at the periphery of the light, raised a hand to her brow, and peered into darkness as thick as a slab of marble. A heavy step nearby made her blood congeal. That wasn't Dexter. Something much larger loomed, watching her. The hairs on her arms stood on end.

"Hello?" Her voice quivered.

Nothing moved, not the wind or the leaves, as she held her breath and listened. Blood sped to her extremities, heightened the tension in her muscles. "Is someone there?" She slid her hand to her waist. Where was her machete? She'd not let it out of her sight the entire time they'd been out here. Why wasn't it on her hip?

Fern took a cautious step backward. Paused and listened. Someone was watching her from the shadows. She knew it, could feel their gaze locked onto hers. She shivered and stepped back again. And crashed into a warm chest. Arms shot around her and squeezed.

She screamed. Yanked her elbow backward and landed a blow to his soft stomach. The arms dropped.

Simon groaned. "Easy, tiger."

Fern spun and punched his shoulder. "You scared me to death!"

"What were you doing?" Simon massaged his abdomen.

"There's someone out there."

His eyes widened. "Where? Who?"

"I don't know." She wrapped her arms around her torso. "I feel like we are being watched."

"Are you sure it's not because of the cameras?"

Maybe. "I don't know." Had she really heard a footstep? Or was it her weary mind playing tricks on her?

Simon swatted her elbow. "Come on. Let's try to get some rest."

"Yeah, you're right. I'm sure Gregory will have another task up his sleeve tomorrow." She shook the tension from her shoulders and returned to the fire. It was her imagination. Had to be. Fern glanced at the black patch again. No one could possibly be out there.

Gregory swiped the card and opened his hotel room door. The initial excitement was waning, and he desperately needed a good night's sleep. He dropped the night vision goggles on the table next to the door. It was a good thing the paranoid man who owned the Army Surplus down the road believed in civilians' rights to owning such things. What luck to have stumbled upon the little shanty the owner called a store.

With Turner monitoring the live feeds and with strict instructions to call should anything unusual occur, Gregory had no doubt he'd have a good night on the comfy mattress. He ordered steak, chocolate dipped strawberries, and buttered rolls for dinner and almost felt guilty eating them while he knew Fern and Simon were starving. Almost.

He took a folder from his briefcase and jotted down notes about the day's events. Step one, place them in an impossible situation. Check. Step two, create an incident to help them bond emotionally. Check. Step three, cast them against a common enemy. Check. Gregory grinned. It was going better than he expected. He made a few notes about the contestants' mental state after days one and two, and then he switched off the light and crawled under the down comforter.

How long would Simon keep the next note a

secret? Gregory had no doubt that he would. If Simon didn't reveal the information himself, Gregory would have to come up with a way to force his hand, as they said. He had a few more tricks up his sleeve. But how far would he need to push them before they broke?

Fern was dozing in the back seat as her father drove them home. Resting on her rolled-up sweatshirt. Flashes behind closed eyelids as other cars passed on the dark country road. A rare trip into town had turned into an all-day outing. Exhilarating. Exhausting. She imagined the headlights reflecting on her retinas were really the dazzling lights of the Ferris wheel they'd seen on the outskirts of town. The fair, she'd been told. It looked like so much fun. Couldn't they stop for a few minutes and watch? No. They didn't have the money, of course. That's why her sweatshirt was four sizes too big. And her shoes were so worn. They never had the money for anything.

A loud crack split the air. Had her dad wrecked their old car? Fern bolted upright. Her head slammed into something hard as her eyes flew open. Where was she? Why couldn't she see anything? Not her hand in front of her face. Not anything at all.

Lightning flashed, lighting up the shelter she and Simon had built. Right. The show. "Simon?" Her words were drowned by a sudden deluge of rain. Seconds later, a steady stream dripped through the A-frame above her. So much for the shelter protecting her. Another flash of lightning lit up the whole world. She jumped. Simon's head peeked through the opening mere inches from hers.

"Did you call for me?" He had to shout to be heard above the storm.

She nodded, forgetting for a moment that he couldn't see her. "Yes! What about the fire?"

"I don't think there's much we can do about it."

Tomorrow morning everything would be soaked. They'd never get another started. They had to do something. But what? Fern's shoulders sagged. There wasn't anything to be done, other than sit and wait and hope for something dry somewhere once daylight broke.

Blinding lightning flashed and thunder split the hiss of the water. Fern's ears rang with the concussion. She felt Simon crawl closer. Brush by her leg, sending her own adrenaline-lightning zipping up her thigh. Her first instinct was to withdraw closer to the tree trunk behind her. Truth was, though, she didn't want to be alone. Chill bumps broke out along the tops of her shoulders and traveled down her arms. The rain had dropped the air temperature. Was it possible to get hypothermia in the middle of summer in East Tennessee? The veterinarian in her knew it was. Crazy as it seemed.

Simon looped his arm around her shoulders and urged her to lean against his warm side. She tensed under his gentle touch. He pressed his cool lips to her ear. "It's okay. It will pass."

She didn't have the energy to tell him it wasn't just the storm that made her tremble.

"What is that noise?"

"Huh?" Fern's eyelids once again darted open. When had she relaxed enough to let them slip closed?

Simon's arm fell away from her. She shivered, and with the next flash she saw he had crawled to the entry of her small shelter.

How could it rain so hard for so long? Had nature always been this way and she'd never noticed it from the safety of her home? Even on the homestead she'd had protection. No electricity but at least a sturdy roof. She leaned her head against the tree, eyes burning to see something. Anything. Then Simon's strong grip was yanking her by the wrist. Out of the shelter. Onto her feet. "What's wrong?"

He didn't answer. Nor did he release her. He paused for a moment, and then dragged her into a run. She thought they headed in the direction they'd hiked in, but she couldn't be sure. How did Simon know which way to go? Where were they going? Why?

He knew it was a bad idea to choose camp on the same elevation as the creek. Why hadn't he argued his point more? That last bolt of lightning revealed a scene that scared him more than it would have before the earlier incidents of the day. He had no desire to almost drown twice in one day.

With Fern's wrist firmly in his grasp, he rushed upward. He hoped he headed in the right direction. They had to get away from the gushing rage that had spilled its banks. No wonder everything close to the creek seemed clean and clear of debris. It was the head of a flash flood zone. All the small sticks, loose dirt, and poorly-rooted plants had been swept away. Only God knew how many times.

His feet slipped on the wet leaves. He crashed to the earth, dragging Fern along with him. She landed squarely on his chest. With his arms wrapped around her, for a moment he forgot they were fleeing a powerful force. It couldn't be as powerful as whatever tingled in his chest. He couldn't see the look on her face, but he could feel the small of her back. The curve of her shoulders. Her wet hair tickling his face. Something deep within him stirred to life.

She shoved hard with both palms and disappeared from his grasp into the darkness thick as the belly of a cave.

"Fern!"

"I'm still here. What is going on?"

What was going on? He could still feel the weight of her body atop his. Found it hard to focus on anything else. He struggled to his feet. "Creek's flooding. We've got to get to higher ground."

With the next flash of lightning, he took his bearings, grabbed her hand, and began climbing the embankment ahead. *Lord, please help us.* Between the exertion and Fern's form pressing against him moments before, the chill that had overtaken him in the shelter melted away. The leaves on the embankment acted like sheets of ice, making a good grip almost impossible. He used his free hand to grab saplings, planting his feet at their bases and dragging Fern up with him. How high did the flash flood water reach? He had no way to be sure, but, at the top of the slope he estimated to be at least twenty-five feet tall, he collapsed against a large tree trunk and bent to catch his breath. Surely this was high enough. Fern's petite hand trembled in his palm.

The storm seemed to be moving on. Its cannon booms and light show climbing over the next mountain ridge. The rain slackened enough to hear himself think but still poured over the cliff, evidenced by the continuous crash. It would take hours for all the water to drain into the creek and travel downstream. "Are you okay?" He squeezed her hand.

"Fine." She yanked her fingers free. "I'm fine."

As the rain retreated, the roar of the creek filled the forest. Angry. Deadly. He never would've guessed their placid, clear water could become such a beast. He slid down the tree and sank to his bottom, realizing for the first time since their start how shaky his legs felt.

"Simon?"

The tremble in Fern's voice gave away her fear. She talked a good game, but he knew inside she was terrified. "I'm still here."

In a moment, her side brushed his as she took a

seat close to his left. Her entire frame shook. He slipped his arm around her shoulders and felt her customary stiffening. Her voice sounded tiny when she spoke again. "Do you think Dexter's okay?"

If the kit was with his mother, maybe. If he'd wandered on his own, probably not. Truth or comfort? "I'm sure he's fine. He's a raccoon. They climb, right?"

Her hair brushed against his shoulder as she nodded. He hoped it was true, but they'd probably never know. He imagined what things would look like once daylight arrived, but for now there was nothing to do but wait for dawn and hope they had something left of their camp.

Chapter 9

Fools! In the storm, Fern and Simon had left all their gear and their diary cams and run away from his cameras. How could they have avoided being recorded by every single one? He was missing their fear. Unacceptable.

"Greg? You still there?" Turner's voice reminded Gregory he was still holding his cell phone.

He gritted his teeth. "Yes."

"Hey, don't shoot the messenger."

"I'm on my way." Gregory ended the call, tossed back his comforter, and placed his feet on the cool floor. What a mess. Those two had broken rules and sacrificed the moments viewers would be truly interested in. Not to mention the ones he needed to see in order to make decisions.

He dressed in the dark, forgoing the jacket and tie. If Simon and Fern had lost all his gear and he had to repurchase everything . . . Slamming his room door behind him, and not caring if he woke the neighbors, he pressed the elevator button twice. Come on. A third press. Why was it so ridiculously slow?

The tires squealed on his Mercedes as he pulled out. He blew through the red light at the intersection. At two in the morning, who would be out in this podunk town, anyway? He'd been lucky to find a hotel that was more than a hovel.

He slid around corners until he made it back to the interstate and easily flew past ninety until he reached the Rarity Mountain exit. The canvas tents of base camp glowed like lanterns in the aftermath of the storm, sides glistening in his headlamps as he swung in and parked beside Turner's Beetle.

Turner met him at the flap with a frown. "How fast did you drive, exactly?"

"Where are they?"

"Okay, no small talk." Turner held the flap open for Gregory to enter.

Two of their cameramen huddled before the huge television. None of the glowing green screens showed a hint of life. Several of the frames revealed the extent of the flood, with creek water only a few feet below the camera positions.

Gregory checked his watch. Only a few hours until dawn. "Get everything ready. As soon as we can see, we find them and remind them what's on the line." Did these two know how to follow rules at all? They certainly didn't act like it.

She hated the feel of his arm on her shoulder. And loved it. Why was she having such a hard time deciding between the two? She needed to put space between them. It was far too intimate.

She needed to stay. Under the wing of his strong arm. The warmth his body shared with hers. The electrical tingle that snaked its way through her veins made her tremble. In the pitch-black, it was easy to imagine the nighttime as a barrier. A bubble keeping her safe from this man she'd only known for a couple of days. Wrapping her in a womb where reality was more like imagination. What she thought, would be what happened. She could control everything with the power of her mind. Surreal illusion.

That night had been dark too. And her thoughts, her willpower, hadn't helped her make the correct decision. Hadn't given her the strength to do what she knew was right.

Fern shrugged Simon's arm away. Huddled her arms closer to her body. It was summer after all. It wasn't like she was going to freeze to death by dawn. She tamped down the stern physician's voice that argued with her logic. The storm was over, and the threat of lightning no longer sizzled in the air. She was fine. Closing her aching eyes, she leaned her head back. A fine mist fell on her face. Surely, daybreak must be soon upon them. How much longer could they wait? Crouched against the rough bark, her feet numb from the angle of her knees. And all their gear. Would they find anything when they returned? Simon had been right to want to build farther from the creek. Could she admit it out loud?

She was a doctor. Supposed to be smarter. More adept. Not to mention her skill set. She'd made a beginner's mistake. One that was going to cost them dearly. She could kick herself. If her feet were still attached to her legs.

Silence stretched between them. Maybe Simon had managed to fall asleep. Though she couldn't imagine how. A gray haze crept into the sky, bringing a thick, foggy morning. Fern stretched and shook the cramps out of her feet. "Come on. Let's see what's left."

Without a word, Simon plodded behind her, sliding on his backside down the embankment half the time. Fern drew up short of camp and gasped. It was as if they hadn't been there at all. No shelter. No fire ring. No nothing. The ground wasn't even charred. The rocks which had seemed so sturdy, so heavy around their fire pit had vanished. The pot, the mosquito net, the bow and arrows, all gone. Their diary cameras. Gregory was going to kill them. At least she had the fire starter around her neck and her machete tucked in her belt. And the cameras in the trees all appeared to be in place. Whether they had drowned or not, she couldn't tell. The task of recovering from this devastating set back well enough to finish the challenge loomed before her. Was it worth the effort? Her body cried with exhaustion. Only two days and it was ready to self-destruct.

The image of a white-plastered building filled her mind's eye. The sign hanging out front bearing her name. Veterinary Services offered by Dr. Fern Strongbow, DVM. She'd never afford it without the prize money. No matter how many years she worked to pay off her student loans.

Then there was Simon. If she left, she'd knock him out of the game too. She was no quitter. No weakling. She squared her shoulders. "I guess we'd better check downstream for our stuff."

Simon grunted. He wouldn't meet her gaze, and she couldn't help but notice how the muscles in his jaw bulged. Was he upset with her? Or the situation? Probably both. And she deserved it. But they could deal with that later. Right now, they had to make a fresh start and reestablish some control over their situation. Picking a handful of dandelion leaves and chickweed from the perimeter somehow still clinging to their piece of earth, she crammed them in her mouth and chewed. "Here. It's not much, but it will give you some vitamins anyway."

He took the proffered greens and munched silently.

She started into the forest, gaze bent on the ground, crossing her fingers the dense vegetation near the creek had caught their gear. It was a long shot but their only hope. Around the first bend in the creek, she spotted the mosquito net tangled in a rhododendron bush. Even from a distance she could tell it was in bad shape. But at least it was there. "Simon! Over here!"

His heavy footsteps approached from somewhere behind and to the right.

"I'll work on this mess. You keep looking for the rest of the gear." Her smile was not met with one in return.

He stomped away, crashing through the rhododendron grove.

She probably should've said please. Or not called to him in the first place. Why was it she was always saying the wrong thing to him? Giving directives instead of asking for help. What had made her call to him in her excitement? It wasn't like she needed his help untangling the net. No, she could do that herself. But, in the moment, she wanted to share her joy at finding it. When was the last time she'd had anyone to share with?

She swiveled her gaze in his direction and a gush of nausea spiked through her. They had to find something to boil water in. Doubled over, she took several deep breaths, swallowed hard, and attempted to stand erect. The nausea still teased her stomach, but she didn't feel its urgency. For the moment, anyway.

It took forever to untangle the net. It had several small holes and one large, gaping one right in its center. It wouldn't be keeping many mosquitoes out at this point. If she had a sewing kit, she could make the necessary repairs. She glanced around. What could she use as thread out here? Something thin but strong. Her life on the homestead hadn't prepared her for this type of improvisation. Magazine pages as toilet paper, sure. Flint and a knife for a fire starter, yes. A magnetized needle and thread for a compass, absolutely. But not this. Not the cloudy, swimming thoughts that refused to line up in her dehydrated brain cells. Not the pangs in her abdomen that never quieted. Not the handsome man whose gentle touch didn't repulse her. None of it.

Fern sank onto a boulder, the net hanging from her limp hand. Moisture filled her eyes. She couldn't let it fall. She needed every precious drop of liquid to stay in her body. Along with the wavering pride each tear would deplete.

The sudden pressure of a warm hand on her shoulder made her jump nearly out of her skin. She swiped at her eyes.

"Look what I found."

Simon's wide grin was contagious, and she found herself smiling despite herself. "The pot. Thank goodness." Kindness radiated from his eyes, drying her tears and melting the edges of her ice walls. How could he treat her sweetly after she'd been harsh and rude? This was a different type of man than she'd ever had the pleasure of meeting.

He filled the pot at the creek, and they returned to camp. Gregory again waited for them.

Great.

He opened his mouth to speak, but Fern cut him off. She was in no mood to hear about his "rules." "Are you going to make this a habit?" She threw the net to the ground and planted her fists on her thinning hips.

Gregory took a step back.

Fern bit her lip to avoid breaking into a smile. She rather enjoyed his discomfort. "Well?"

His eyebrows creased together. He matched her stance. "Dr. Strongbow, I'll advise you not to take that tone with me. It will do you well to remember who's in charge here."

"Some head honcho you are. We nearly drowned last night!"

"The weather is not under my control. You are the one who chose to erect your camp so close to the creek. The blame lies squarely on your shoulders, Fern."

Her chest deflated. He was right. Simon was right. She'd been wrong. It was all her fault.

"And, to top it off, you two didn't bother to grab any of your gear. I presume my cameras are gone."

She nodded but couldn't meet his gaze.

"This is your last chance, understand me?"

It was her father lecturing her all over again. That night when she'd stayed out too late. Way past curfew and couldn't bring herself to tell him why. The shame burned her cheeks that night hotter than it did now. And she had survived that.

She could survive this too.

She raised her gaze and stared directly into Gregory's flaming eyes. "Our last chance, eh? I dare you to find two people who would put up with such nonsense. You have no idea what it's like out here. We are starving and thirsty and exhausted. I suppose you'll be wanting this back." Fern held out the wrecked mosquito net. He didn't move to take it. "And you haven't even given us another clue so that we have a chance of getting out of this horrible predicament."

Gregory's gaze darted behind her and he smirked. "Haven't told her yet, Simon?"

Fern spun on her heels. "Told me what?"

The note was gone. Melted into tiny shreds in his pocket by the rain water. He had memorized its simple text, though. He squirmed under Fern's intense glare.

"I brought you two new cameras. Don't lose them this time." Gregory started to turn but paused. "You know what, keep them with you at all times. And use them more often. You signed up to be on a television show. That can't happen unless we have footage." He smacked the diary cams onto a fallen log, grabbed what was left of the mosquito net, and retreated in the direction of base camp.

Fern's gaze never broke from boring a burning hole through his forehead, even as Gregory spoke and stomped away. It was Simon's turn for the hot seat. But he couldn't explain Seth. Not yet. Maybe not ever. If he'd known that would be a part of this dumb contest, would he have ever signed up? He could go home. Follow Gregory into the forest and be sleeping in his own bed with a full belly. And an empty wallet. And crushed self-esteem. And no prospects whatsoever.

"We need to find a new place to set up camp."

"Oh, no. You aren't getting out of it that easy. What is Gregory talking about?"

He hadn't expected changing the subject to work. He had to do something to get away from Fern's lava-launching eyes. "It's nothing." He needed to stall. "Let's gather new shelter materials and head up the embankment to where we hunkered out the storm last night." He risked a small smile.

She quickly stamped it off his face. "I'm not moving from this spot until you tell me. Now."

Heat boiled up his neck, scalding his jugular as it climbed. "Fine! I have the next clue, okay? Is that what you want to hear?"

Fern's fisted hands fell limply to her sides. "Why didn't you tell me?"

The hurt marring her beautiful face was too much to bear. His voice softened. "Because it's not a dare this time. It's a truth." He sucked in a breath and mentally encouraged his wobbly knees. "And truth is, I'm scared."

"Scared of what?"

"The way you'll feel about me after I tell you the story." He'd hoped to take his time easing into the telling of his past. No. He'd hoped to avoid it altogether, hadn't he? Out here where no one would casually bring it up, deep down he'd wanted Fern never to find out. He should have seen Gregory's manipulation coming.

"Oh."

"I get the distinct impression that unless I tell you, we won't get another clue pointing us toward the prize."

"Then tell me. It can't be that bad."

"You'd be surprised."

"Oh, come on. Let me guess. You're a murderer or something, right?" She laughed but sobered quickly when he didn't join her. "Simon?"

He cleared his throat, shoved his hands into his damp pockets, and nodded.

"What? You can't be serious." She took a step back.

His Jell-O knees were going to buckle and leave him flat on his face if he didn't sit down. Why was this so hard? He'd talked about his past before. With employers, his family, and his lawyers. It's not like he'd never spoken the words. Why was it so different that he was breaking the news to a dark-eyed beauty whose frown ate at him? "We'd better sit down." He led the way to the log where Gregory had placed the cameras, noting the distance Fern placed between them.

"I was in prison for nine years, four months, fifteen days, and seven hours. For vehicular homicide. It was an accident, but it was my fault. The boy who . . . died was only eight." He'd never forget Seth's face. Or the way the bicycle had been crumpled like a discarded paper clip. Never outlive the guilt. "My brother Lance was with me." Simon would never forget the look on Lance's face, either, the blanched cheeks and hollow, scared eyes.

Fern scooted a few more inches away. "How did you . . . ? I mean, how can you be here? You killed someone and you're out free, walking around? What about the boy's parents? What about justice?"

A barbed sword pierced his heart. She was reacting exactly how he feared. He reached for her hand, but she yanked it away. "I'm sorry. For what happened. For having to tell you. For not telling you from the start. Don't you have any secrets you'd rather keep buried?"

Secrets? Only two. She wavered for a fraction of a second. No, Simon hadn't been honest with her. He'd been hiding the clue from her and deceiving her about his true nature. How could Gregory partner her with a felon? A murderer, no less.

She couldn't do this.

If she'd had moments of feeling safe with Simon, they were over now. Forever. There wasn't any safety under the shelter of his protective, muscly arms. None. How would she force herself to finish the contest? She flew to her feet, grabbed her new diary cam, and marched into the forest. She needed to get busy. Maybe if she occupied her body, her mind would cease its reckless reeling. Its careening off a cliff of fear and worry. They were losing daylight, and they had new shelters to build.

She needed to get away from him. She scampered up the incline from the previous night and found the top surprisingly level. Simon would follow her, she knew, but for the moment the solitude refreshed her weary mind. Thoughts of how to continue and how to sleep in the empty forest with a murderer could come later. They would come, and she would figure this out, because she wasn't letting some crazy director and some handsome ex-con stop her from her dream.

With her machete, she chopped down saplings and dragged them to a spot at the base of a twin-trunked beech tree with full, swooping branches. She propped the diary cam on a limb and flipped open its screen. A slip of paper drifted to the ground. Her heart paused as she bent to pick it up. What was Gregory's next mission?

TRUTH.

Your turn.

Her turn for what? No, no, no. Not that. She brought her hand to her gaping mouth. There was no way. She'd never told anyone. Not a single soul. Gregory couldn't have found out. Her skeletons were too deeply hidden.

But what else could it mean? Other than this, the most painful, horrible memory she possessed, she had no real secrets. Nothing that compared to Simon's earlier confession. Other than that one. Two intertwined ones if someone were counting. She shook her head. Gregory didn't know about that. He had to mean something else. She crammed the note in her pocket. It wouldn't hurt to spend a few hours contemplating its meaning. Would it?

"This is my second diary cam entry." Fern cleared her throat. "I've officially slept next to a murderer." She chuckled. "Notice the distinction. Next to. Yesterday was hard. Learning about Simon's past almost sent me home." She aimed her gaze directly into the lens and, hopefully, into the eyes of the viewers coming in a few months. "I will not let that deter me." Gregory would see. She could do this. If only she could figure out what the next clue meant. Other than her initial impression, she could think of nothing.

"I finished my shelter today." She panned the camera so viewers could see it sitting beneath its quiet tree. "And we started Simon's." Where was Simon, anyway? No doubt scouting game again. She hoped he found something, anything edible. But she wasn't going to bet on it.

A rustling sounded behind her, in the scrubby brush beneath a smattering of oaks. Dexter? Even though days had passed since his disappearance, a part of her couldn't stop wondering if he was okay and if she'd see him again.

She moved to the tangle of green and peered into its shadowed depths. Instead of an adorable raccoon she hoped to find, she startled a nesting Titmouse. It burst forth, zipping past her head in a flurry of dark gray feathers and loud screeches. Leaving behind six pearly, vulnerable eggs.

Food.

Life.

Life-giving food. Which was the most important, in this moment, in hers and Simon's states? The eggs, though tiny, were packed with protein that her body desperately needed. Yet, as a veterinarian her responsibilities to animal-kind were different than others'. She had made a vow to help them. It was a far cry from the homestead, where she'd grown up with butchering right in front of her face every single day. Once she walked away from her parents' farm, she walked away from killing too. Yes, she ate meat, but there was a distance, a coldness, an impersonal nature to buying something in a plastic and foam package from the store. Whereas, if she stole these little eggs and dropped them into the boiling water on the fire, she was personally, firsthand responsible for their death.

And she had met the mother. All but looked her in the eye.

"Fern? What are you doing?" Simon's voice called from the direction of the creek.

She let the branches snap into place. "Nothing.

What's up?"

"I caught a few crawdads. Ready for dinner?" The exuberance in his voice lifted her spirits.

Though Simon didn't know it, he was her hero again, saving her from the agonizing decision of killing the innocent chicks hiding inside their cream-colored shells. And it wasn't like the eggs would magically move. If they couldn't find another food soon, she would return for them.

"Diary cam entry number five.

"Fern is still acting strange. I can't believe she hasn't left yet. It's absolutely, beyond the shadow of a doubt, clear that she is terrified of me. I don't know why I thought it'd be any different this time.

"You know, America, it's dumb how you treat us ex-felons. Sure some of us are bad guys, but you don't even try to figure out which one is which." Why was he saying any of this? It wasn't like it would change anything. It was making him feel better though. "You know, the things that happened in my past aren't a total calculation of who I am. My grand sum is more than equal to the parts you see.

"For example, how many people know I loved to sing in the choir when I was a kid? Or that I once ran over a frog's leg with my bicycle and nursed him back to health with popsicle sticks and dead flies?" His stomach growled at the thought of frog legs. He didn't even like them, but they were food. Glorious food. The crawdad supper two nights ago was long gone. And every sign of life at the creek had vanished. It was as if a memo had been sent out to every crawling, slithering, swimming, and hopping thing to hide, run, escape the big, bad hunter with no weapon besides a limb.

A branch popped in the darkness beyond the firelight. Fern was back. The time for revelations, over. He pushed the off button and laid the camera at his side. Another long night awaited. Would tomorrow be any better at all?

"Diary cam entry number six.

"I have no idea if Fern is keeping up with her entries like Gregory wants us too. I hope so, because this isn't easy on me and I'm doing it." Maybe that's where she'd been going every day. He shrugged. "Anyway, I have a sneaking suspicion my partner has the next clue and is holding out on me. Paranoia? Maybe. I am so hungry it's insane. I can't remember a time I've ever wanted a good meal more." Images of deep fried foods of any sort floated in his weary brain. For a moment, he imagined he could even smell French fries and McDonald's chicken nuggets. "I've got nothing new to add to the diary today. There hasn't been much sign of game, though I've looked every day. Not sure what I'd kill 'em with if I did find them." He snickered. "Maybe I'd be lucky. I doubt it, but I can't seem to stop looking nonetheless. All right, see you tomorrow."

Chapter 10

How had a few hours turned into a full week? Surely Simon must be wondering what was taking Gregory so long to produce another clue. Had he figured out that she was hiding something? She glanced toward him as he stoked the fire in front of his shelter several paces away. He smiled at her, and she ducked her head, her fingers nimbly weaving a new fish basket trap with grapevines she had been soaking in the creek for a day and a half.

Their week had passed slowly. The camera crew had moved all the cameras to their new camp location, and she and Simon had been trying to remember to keep up with their personal diaries and GoPros. She'd not managed to do it much. If she was "confessing" to the camera, she might accidentally let it slip that she was lying to Simon each moment of each day.

She didn't know that she'd ever get used to the

idea that her every movement was caught on film and sent to Gregory for possible television airing. The one thing that kept her going was the thought of that veterinary hospital with her name on it. She'd come way too far to quit.

They'd finally finished Simon's shelter and had focused on keeping the fire going and boiling water to stay hydrated. She wasn't comfortable with Simon's presence per se, especially at night when she closed her eyes and felt most vulnerable. But keeping her machete close at all times had helped. If he decided to revisit his past tendencies toward violence, she'd be ready.

She checked the nest every day, knowing in her heart the longer she waited, the more formation the babies acquired. The harder it would be to eat them, and the less tasty. Were they her security blanket? Guaranteed food when she couldn't make it one more second. Sure, that was it. A backup policy against starvation.

There had been no sign of Dexter, or any animals in their camp for that matter. The only sustenance they'd been able to produce had been handfuls of tiny trout fingerlings caught with a piece of the mosquito net Simon found snagged in the rhododendron bush. These they had dropped whole into the pot, added a few greens, and eaten as a watery-fishy stew. It wasn't nearly enough nutrition. For either of them.

Fern flexed her skinny fingers. Her forearms were someone else's. They had to be. Skeletal in nature after only ten days in the wild. The blackberry bush she'd discovered yesterday on the far side of their creek had been a welcome fresh, sweet taste to both their palates. But they'd have to eat a thousand of them to gain any real nutritional value. Her mouth watered at the thought of warm blackberry cobbler topped with vanilla bean ice cream. That had been happening a lot over the last several days. Random thoughts of mouth-watering food that only made the stomach pain all the more unbearable.

Losing Simon's bow and arrows had been a huge blow to their ability to garner food from the inhospitable landscape. Wouldn't Gregory see their suffering and provide them with something helpful soon? Surely he was getting tired of the sluggishness of the show by now.

Her heart picked up its pace. What would Gregory do if she didn't fess up soon? Would he force her hand? Of course he would. He was a vicious, controlling man whose one goal was great television. She sighed and rolled her eyes. She wasn't ready. Would she ever be?

As the sun sank behind the now-familiar western horizon, Simon added another small stone to the pile he'd begun erecting next to his shelter to track their days. "Something's got to give." He mumbled to himself, but Fern caught the ache in his voice. She felt it herself. The longing for a comfortable bed. A shower. A hot meal. An escape from the feeling that eyes were on them at all times.

Simon broke a stick over his knee.

Fern jumped. She'd been doing that a lot the last few days too. Each night they'd settled in, she had the feeling of someone watching. Waiting in the shadows. Her nerves felt like severed power cords. Frayed wires that reduced the capacity to send messages from her brain to her body.

They'd never manage to survive another twenty days like this.

Fern drew a deep breath. She had to come clean. The anger she'd felt at Simon had long evaporated as she herself hid a clue in her pocket and refused to fess up. She understood now why he had kept his own secret quiet. And he only did it for two days. Simon was going to hate her when she finally told him. Each minute that passed only made revealing her treachery that much harder. The burden of guilt weighed on her empty stomach. If she confessed, bared her skeleton, maybe Gregory would send food tomorrow. Tomorrow they could be eating something besides minnows and berries. And she wouldn't have to boil the eggs that were more chick than egg at this point. "I have the clue, Simon."

His head jerked. "What? How?"

"I'm a terrible partner. I've had it for a week."

"You what?" His voice roared in the quiet forest, a giant's bellow that made her tremble and touch the machete at her waist with shaking fingers.

Tears welled in her eyes. "I'm so sorry. I know why you couldn't tell me right away about your Truth clue. I'm sorry." She wrung her hands together and refused to meet his gaze.

Simon chuckled, softly at first, but his horse-laugh soon filled the forest.

She grinned nervously. "Why are you so happy?"

"I have no idea. Maybe it's because I thought you acting withdrawn and scared the last ten days was because you were petrified of me. Now I know. It's because you have skeletons too. Don't you?"

Fern nodded. They were almost as bad as his. She had no right to judge him. She'd just done a better job of hiding her shame all these years. She glared at him. This was hard enough already without him laughing his face off.

He tried hard to stifle his laughter with his massive palm. "I'm sorry, Fern. It's not funny. I'm so tired. And so hungry. I don't think my brain is firing on all cylinders."

"I know what you mean." She was riding an emotional roller coaster between tears and anger, giddiness out of nowhere, and returning to tears and hopelessness. Their bodies direly needed sustenance and rest.

"All right, what's your *truth*?"

Her desire to be free of the suffering outweighed her ability to keep her tongue quiet any longer. "When I was sixteen, I knew I wanted more than what my parents had." A reservoir burst inside her, words gushing forward faster than she could breathe. "Not that I didn't love them or appreciate all they did for me, mind you. And I loved living on the homestead. But I hated the fact that we were poor. More than that, though, I felt like I was trapped. Like my parents' decision to live life the way they had chosen meant keeping me stifled." She shuddered. She'd never said these words aloud. What would her parents think of her if they ever found out? Drawing a deep breath, she dug her fingernails into her opposing palm. "I wanted to be a veterinarian from the earliest memories I have. We never saved our sick animals. We couldn't afford to. And it broke my heart, knowing that if we could call a vet they wouldn't have had to die.

"So I got a job working at a diner in town. I hiked to work every afternoon when I finished my homeschool studies. It was weird. My parents were disappointed. But they were hippies." Fern giggled. "They have this way about them. This way of letting you know that whatever you choose to be, it must be in the 'Universe's' plans to create you that way. This laid-back, accepting nature. I don't know how to explain it. Because they wished, and still do wish, that I hadn't ever left, but they never tried to talk me out of it." She took a steadying breath. "I wish that I hadn't taken that job either. A few months after I started, the night shift manager took a liking to me. He filled my head with all the things a young woman wants to hear. Wants to believe. We dated for a while and one night he offered me a ride home, but we didn't make it right away."

Fern's throat constricted. She couldn't do this.

Couldn't revisit that dark night and what it led to.

"Fern . . ." The sadness in Simon's voice gave her a measure of courage.

"I should never have thought he cared about me, I suppose. Not really. But I was young. And, oh, so inexperienced. It wasn't until years later it dawned on me how sheltered I'd been on the homestead. Sure, I learned to hold a gun and a bow at the ripe old age of four. Learned how to dress a deer and harvest chickens. All those life skills that were imperative on the homestead.

"No one ever taught me how to handle myself around a man. I thought I knew the kind of person he was. I didn't." She hugged her arms tighter around her midsection. "The look in his eyes, I'll never forget it. Never forget the way it made me feel powerless. I let him convince me everything would be okay. That he loved me. I never really agreed, but I didn't put up a fight either. I figured this is what love led to. Natural, right? But it didn't feel that way to me. Nothing about it was right. It was so, so wrong that sometimes I still can't believe it was real. That I let myself fall for his lies and tricks and falsehoods. And that will forever be my first memory of . . . of . . ." Her voice broke. She hiccupped as tears poured down her face. "I've never told a soul."

"Fern." What could he say to help her muddle

through the pain? If he could get his hands on that boss of hers, whoever he was, he'd make him think twice about taking advantage of the amazing, resilient young Fern he knew she'd been. A man that took advantage of a naïve child was no man at all. "I can't imagine."

And Gregory. Why would that jerk make her confess such an awful part of her past? His was public record. He had done something wrong and he'd deserved to be punished. But poor Fern. She'd done nothing to deserve the scars she'd received. Nothing to deserve a memory that shouldn't be. Real love was different than what she'd experience. Tenderness. Desire that reached deeper than physical needs. Not that he had any experience with real love himself. But he could see it in the way his parents loved one another. The way his grandparents had loved each other for more than fifty years.

Her body quaked as sobs wracked her thin frame. His arms ached to hold her. Somehow, he knew they would be unwelcome. No doubt she relived every moment of that night. He wouldn't add to her discomfort. *Lord, please, I beg you, help Fern. I can't imagine what she's going through. What she went through.*

When had he last prayed so often? He had found himself talking with God all week. Thinking about his brothers and his parents and praying safety over them. Praying for help and stamina for himself and Fern. It was a comfort. Why had he ever stopped talking to the Creator of the moon and stars?

He moved to Fern's side, careful not to touch her body, and gently took her hand in his. He vowed to sit with her as long as it took her to work through the memories of, no doubt, the worst part of her life.

"She's hiding something." Gregory tapped the monitor.

Turner leaned in. "How can you tell?"

"We'll have to push her harder. Until she tells the full truth."

"Did you know about her past?"

"Yes."

"Why would you make her confess something so horrible on national television?"

"Drama?"

Turner's eyes widened. But Gregory didn't have to explain himself. Not to Turner. Not to anyone. In the end, everyone would see. The results would be priceless

"How did you know?"

"I had a feeling. What is important is getting her to admit the rest of the story." She would break. Gregory would make sure of it. "Prepare tomorrow's challenge. I want the drone sent at dawn with their instructions. And tell the crew to begin their trek out to the camp as soon as they can see their hands in front of their faces, as they say."

Turner sighed and leaned back in his padded

swivel chair. "Gregory, are you sure about this?"

"Not your call to make. I'm the director. The financier. Everything."

"Some of the crew is getting antsy. There have been . . . rumors."

Gregory snickered. "There always are when history is being made. You can tell them they either do their jobs or they can leave. Money will buy their replacements." He squinted his eyes tighter. "Yours too."

Turner's eyebrows shot up. He opened his lips but clamped them shut again.

Gregory's cell phone jingled in his shirt pocket. He whipped it out and checked the caller ID. "I've got to take this. Print the instructions and get the drone ready." He walked out of the canvas tent into the dark night. Millions of stars glimmered overhead. The Milky Way stretched across the perfectly clear sky. He took a deep breath and pushed the green button. "Hi, Pops."

"You have the nerve to send someone to pick me up? I asked you. Not some intern who doesn't know how to drive."

"I'm still on vacation—"

"Vacation? Who gave you permission for that? I certainly didn't authorize it."

His father's voice was reaching the high octave Gregory had come to associate with a blood red face and bulging neck veins. "I needed a break, Pops."

"A break! A break? I'm off slaving away to build

our company—your company someday if you play your cards right—and you needed a break?"

Not really, he hadn't. Not a break. Something different. In fact, he was more stressed with the television show work than he'd been in ages. But he couldn't let Pops know that. Besides it was a different kind of stress. A rewarding, fulfilling day-to-day kind that, for the first time in his life, led to smiles and weary sleep. He loved it. Part of him longed to call Jenny and tell her how he had finally broken free from his father's grasp and started his dream. Well, sort of broken free. More like started a fissure, anyway.

They only had three weeks of filming left. Maybe less if Fern would cooperate. "I'm sorry, Pops. Really."

"Sorry isn't what I want to hear." Pops took a ragged breath Gregory could hear through the phone. "You will be here bright and early tomorrow morning, or there will be dire consequences. You understand me?"

Tomorrow? How could he be there tomorrow?

"Gregory? You will answer me."

How could he not be there tomorrow? His father's tone threatened to slice his earlobe off through the phone. He hung his head and sutured up the fissure. "Yes, sir."

Dawn brought the darkest sky they'd seen since

the evening of the flood. Fern sighed. *Not more rain. Please not more rain.* Who was she directing that hope to? Certainly not God. Was she? She had never prayed that she could remember. Yes, she'd had thoughts directed to some higher power or something. But her parents had always said that the universe was in control. Fate. And Karma. And all that jazz. Fern hadn't really believed that, but she didn't exactly believe in an omnipotent, omniscient God either. She'd noticed Simon praying a time or two. At least she figured that must be what he was doing when he bent his head and closed his eyes. How would she know what praying looked like? Or felt like.

The hum of Gregory's drone approached their new campsite. The little white flier sat down in the periphery, carrying underneath it another folded-up paper. "Simon, you awake yet?"

He moaned from the direction of his shelter.

"We have another clue."

"Great."

"Your enthusiasm is palpable."

He chuckled.

"What do you think our director has for us today? Another murder attempt?" Fern clamped her hand to her mouth. She hadn't meant to use that word. How insensitive could she be?

"Probably."

She released the breath she held. Simon's voice didn't sound angry, just slurred with grogginess. "I'll see what it says." When she crawled out of her shelter and rose to her feet, the dizziness that had plagued her for days set in. She stumbled, caught herself on a sapling with a weak grip, and closed her eyes. *Please let these instructions lead us to food.*

"*DARE*

Today's a journey for the not-so-faint of heart.
You must each play a part.
But Fern will be in the lead.
There's a compass to guide you.
To the South for two,
Head East by the gnarly tree.
When the day is done,
And you find the sun,
You will eat.

Begin your preparations now. The crew will be there shortly. Don't leave without them."

Simon had come to her side while she read aloud. Her own secrecy and then forced confession had taken some of the tension from between them. Simon had somehow known what she needed and had not pushed any of the boundaries between them. She could stand next to him without feeling like fleeing. He took a step closer and the irksome butterflies she still hadn't managed to snub out awoke.

He rubbed his hands together. "We will eat? Like real food?"

She giggled at the adorable expression of excitement on his face. Her stomach rumbled at the thought of real food. "I hope so. But what do you think it all means?"

"South for two, right? Two miles maybe?"

She nodded. "Probably right." But how could they hike two miles? Her legs were jelly and her head spun every time she exerted herself. Was Gregory nuts?

"We'd better boil some water and drink as much as we can. It looks like it will be a long day."

She heard the camera crew approaching long before she saw them. Their noisy steps and irritated voices echoed off the rim and into camp. Her little titmouse darted out of the bush, flitting into the tree overhead as tiny peeps echoed from below. Fern's chicks had hatched sometime overnight, apparently. She smiled. It was a wonderful thing she didn't eat them, their tiny voices reminded her, bringing joy to their growing-more-somber-everyday campsite. Did the bird know where Dexter was? Too bad she couldn't ask her.

Simon lifted his head. "Ready?"

She brought her focus back to the matter at hand, with some difficulty considering her sludgy synapses. "I guess I have to be. Sure wish he'd sent something to eat before we have to hike to who knows where."

Simon nodded and rose to his feet. He held out his hand to help her up.

She took it. The usual blackening of the outer rims dimmed her vision. She swayed and Simon caught her to his chest, wrapping his hardened arms around her midsection.

"You okay?"

Squeezing her eyes shut, she longed to lean into his chest. To nuzzle her head into the nape of his neck. There was safety there. Had been from the first time he'd tried to comfort her. Could she trust it? Trust him? All the people she'd ever let get close had let her down. Why would Simon be any different?

Her eyelids flew open. She tugged free of his grip and brushed her shirt with trembling fingers.

The camera crew emerged from the dense brush of the forest seconds later. Heat crawled up her face, burning her cheeks in what she knew would be a bright blush. Even though the embrace was innocent enough, it probably wouldn't look that way on camera.

Chapter 11

They'd been hiking for hours. It felt like it, anyway. Simon's legs trembled each time he was forced to descend even the minutest bump in the forest floor. As if they could no longer support his weight. His lungs burned with each breath. Sweat poured from his forehead, ran down his temples, and tickled his neck. The camera crew tagged along behind, save for the one man who must have drawn the short straw and was tasked with walking backward ahead of them. How the man hadn't already fallen, Simon couldn't figure. They must really dislike him to submit him to such a strenuous task. Simon chuckled. Like Gregory must despise him and Fern. They'd been tortured for ten and a half days, with no end in sight. But maybe there was a meal at the end of this day's task. One could only hope.

"Seen any 'gnarly trees'?" His voice sounded

gravelly to his own ears.

"No. You?"

"Uh-uh. We have to be about there. You sure we're still headed in the right direction?"

Fern cocked her head to the side, studying the compass she raised to shoulder height. "Yep."

Her curt reply told him he'd stepped on her toes. Again. It seemed to be her standard reaction in times of stress. He chose to let it roll over him. All thoughts were consumed by food and water. And rest. And maybe a steak topped with a Parmesan sauce and onions sautéed in butter. And a giant yeast roll with honey butter. And a cold Mountain Dew to wash it all down. Drool pooled in his dry mouth. He shook his head. The best he could hope for today would probably be some granola or a protein bar. But it would beat minnow or earthworm stew.

They stopped while Fern checked her heading once more, and Simon sank to the ground to catch his breath. The camera crew pulled long slugs from their canteens. Sweat soaked through their t-shirts. Simon glanced down at his soiled clothing. He and Fern must stink. Though, when he'd caught her in his arms, all he'd caught a whiff of was an earthy scent that made him want to press his nose to her scalp. Or to the soft circle below her earlobe. Where the flesh must be soft and sweet. Heat flushed his abdomen. He had to find a way to get those kinds of thoughts out of his head. After the confession of her traumatic past, the last thing she needed was for him to fantasize about her soft skin. How it might feel to taste the hollow of her neck. How it might feel to . . . He shook his head.

"Simon?"

He snapped to attention. "Huh?"

"Did you hear me?"

"No. Sorry. What?"

"The gnarly tree. I see it!"

Her excitement gave him strength to return to his feet. She pointed to a short redbud about a hundred yards ahead and down a slight incline. Its limbs jutted at odd angles from a stunted trunk. "I'd call that gnarly. Lead the way."

Fern nearly trotted down the hill and fingered the low-hanging leaves. "I've never seen a redbud quite like it. Have you?"

Simon shook his head.

"It's like a great hand came down and twisted the trunk, and then crinkled up all the branches. Weird."

He wanted to answer. To tell her it if there was a great hand, it was God's. No one else could create something so uniquely beautiful. But his mouth clove together like it was filled with sticky peanut butter.

"Are you okay?"

No. Had he answered aloud? Why did it feel like his feet were detached from the rest of his body? The ground rose up to meet him in a clouded blur of color. His head, feeling as if it were insulated inside a plastic bag, slammed into the ground. He couldn't breathe any more of the thick, hot air. The concern in Fern's voice made him want to struggle to get up. But his body wouldn't cooperate. A sharp pain streaked from the base of his skull down his neck. A crowd of faces hovered between him and the sky. Why wouldn't his limbs respond when he told them to get up?

"Give him water," one said.

"Gregory'll kill us," another answered.

"I don't care! I ain't going to jail because Gregory murdered someone on this stupid show," another, deeper voice replied.

Cool metal pressed against his cracked lips. The sweetest, purest water he was sure he'd ever tasted flowed into his parched mouth, stripped away the crackly feeling from the surface of his tongue as it washed over, and slid down his scratchy throat. The tempter pulled the canteen away. No! He needed more. A groan escaped him.

Fern's proud cheekbones and Jacobean eyes came into focus above him as his vision began to clear. He blinked. Blinked again. "More water. Please." He'd never begged for a thing in his life. He'd gladly give up every ounce of pride he had right now for one more sip. She turned away, her long, dark hair cascading over his face. With the weakness in all his limbs, he was powerless to wipe it from his cheeks. He didn't want to anyway. If anything, he longed to pull her closer. To submerge his exhausted eyes and mouth in the depths of that gorgeous, silken hair.

"We can't give him more," the first crewman replied.

She disappeared from view. He heard the water

slosh in the metal container and in a few short seconds Fern pressed it to his lips again. "Drink slowly." She cupped the back of his head with her free hand. He could imagine the scathing look she shot the man who refused him more water. She'd said he was her hero, a moment he wouldn't take for granted or soon forget, but, really, she was the champion. The no-nonsense fighter. The gorgeous warrior with tempting curves.

He drank greedily, staring into her eyes so close to his face. Her lips compressed with concern for him. A few inches and he could meet them.

She pulled the canteen away and used the hem of her shirt to wipe his cheek where a drip of water trailed through his beard and to his ear. "Better?"

He nodded. Never had he seen someone so lovely. "You're beautiful, Fern. Do you know that?"

Her eyes widened like those of a newborn fawn, dark pools of compassion. And fear. A smile played at the corner of her lips. "You've got a concussion."

"I'm fine. Help me up."

Between Fern and the camera crew, he managed to make it onto his feet again. Woozy and with a pounding head, but his vision seemed completely normal and no dizziness accompanied his return to vertical posture. "Thanks, guys."

The man with the deep voice gripped his shoulder. "You can't mention this to Gregory. Not ever. Okay?"

"Deal."

"Okay, boys, turn the cameras back on." Deep-voice and the other two flicked the switches on the sides of their cameras, bringing them out of sleep mode.

"Let's rest, Simon. A few more minutes. Okay?"

"I'm fine." He took a step and stumbled into Fern's side. "Okay, maybe a minute more."

She glanced at Simon again for the dozenth time since they'd resumed their hike. His pale face still glistened with a clammy sheen that made her stomach clench. The small amount of water the camera crew had given him apparently was enough to keep him on his feet. For now. But he was badly dehydrated. They were going to have to do something soon. *Please let there be food and water ahead.* She checked the compass again. Still headed due east. How long were they supposed to trod through the forest? Would they know when to stop?

The next part of the clue talked about the day being done, but the sun beat down from its afternoon position, still hours before dark. Simon would need water in order to make it back to camp. So would she. She struggled to hide the swirling feeling blurring her vision and clouding her head. There was no way they could push until dusk without rest and hydration.

An hour later, the distinguishable sound of water falling drifted to them on a slight breeze. She smiled when she looked over her shoulder and found that

Simon had perked up. He nodded and motioned for her to continue. Fern emerged through the trees to find herself standing on the edge of a vertical drop, similar to the one above their camp. Higher, though. Much, much higher. A creek flung itself from the rock wall to her left, falling over a hundred feet. She'd wager it was their creek many miles downstream from camp.

Between where she stood and the bank opposite lay a massive hemlock tree, either end perched solidly on the bluff face, creating a bridge of sorts. It appeared that the creek followed a path down massive stair-steps made of rock ledges at varying elevations. If they could view it from a giant's perspective towering in the sky, they'd see the first drop was above their camp. How many lie between camp and here, she had no way to tell, but clearly the creek gained steam as it descended, because the roar of the fall drowned out all the other forest sounds. Her mouth watered. If only they could reach the delicious spray.

"What now?"

Simon's voice close to her ear sent a rocket of chills tiptoeing down her spine. The heat from his body flooded her back, making speech a challenge. "I don't know."

"Let me guess. East is over that?" He pointed at the tree bridge.

She nodded.

"I think Gregory really is trying to kill us."

No one would be dumb enough to commit murder on camera. Would they? She cast her glance around hoping to find some sort of tether system. Harnesses and ropes. Anything to make the crossing safer, but she found nothing.

It would have to be her who crossed. She refused to let Simon risk falling again. Not after he'd scared the daylights out of her at the redbud. She leaned over the side and took in the distance to the ground. No way he'd survive that if he fell. Neither would she, but she could control herself. If she sent him across, she couldn't do a thing about it if he got woozy again.

"You stay here." She hoped her firm tone told him it wasn't up for debate.

"I can't—"

"I won't argue. I'll get over there, find whatever it is Gregory left for us, and be right back." She pointed at the cameraman with the slightest build. "You." He jumped. "You're coming with me. You two, stay here."

She didn't wait to see if they were going to comply. Instead, she turned her back, cinched her shoelaces tighter, and placed one foot on the tree and pressed. It seemed steady. She should be able to shimmy right across. It was certainly wide enough. Without another glance downward, she clambered onto the top. Water sprayed in a fine mist from the fall, coating the ridged, lined bark. Great. As if this task weren't bad enough already without being slippery. She flung her arms out for balance and picked a spot on the far bank to focus on. One step in front of the other. Simple. The spray from the water, at least, felt good on her face.

About a dozen steps in, too far for either bank to be of use should she slip, her heart leapt into her throat. She was walking across a tree trunk over a gorge. Had she lost her mind? Her throat constricted. What was she doing? Half a million dollars wasn't worth her life. Hadn't she told Gregory that a few days ago about Simon? Her feet froze in place.

"Fern!"

Simon's shout reached her ears. She pressed her eyelids closed. She couldn't do this. But it was too late to turn around. She could sense the cameraman close behind her. They were both going to die if she didn't find a way to move forward. *I can't!*

She wanted to sink to her knees, hug the tree, and refuse to move. Become a proverbial bump on a log. If she never took another step, she'd never fall. Just cling to the tree until the end of time. Right. That made a lot of sense. She snickered. Her eyes snapped open. She drew a deep, ragged breath and blew it out through her flared nostrils. Risking one glance downward, she inched her foot forward. Her grip held for a second before it slipped sideways on the slime-covered trunk.

"Fern!" Simon's screams from the bank echoed around her. Time stopped as her foot flailed into empty space. She was going to fall to her death. Her right leg buckled, sending her crashing to her knee. Pain lanced her patella. Air whooshed from her lungs in a muffled groan. Her hands grappled to find something, anything, to grab onto as her body twisted and tried to follow her flailing foot. Her hand found a hold on a thick branch. She grasped it for dear life. Pulled hard. Righted herself on top of the massive, round trunk. Her legs slid around either side, like a saddle atop a horse. She'd wanted to hug the tree, hadn't she?

She leaned forward, gripping the trunk with her legs so tightly they tingled, and planted her elbows on the rough bark. She hung her head. That was too close. She craned her neck carefully to peer behind her. Simon and the cameramen watched with mouths hanging open. All three of them. The man she'd directed to come with her didn't look like he'd tried to come at all. Then whose presence had she felt behind her, urging her to move forward?

Every fiber of her body trembled as she gave a tentative thumbs up to the guys. She didn't have a voice left to try to speak. It lay at the bottom of the gorge. But she would make it across. Even if it was crazy, just to know she could. Adrenaline spiked her blood and gave her the energy to scoot, inch by inch, forward across the remaining distance like a caterpillar slowly humping along the log.

She flung herself onto the far bank. Never had the ground felt so good beneath her. Who cared that her forearm bled where it had scraped against a sharp stump of a branch? Or that her knee tingled with the oncoming bruise? She was alive. For the moment. And hungrier than ever. She flipped the GoPro on her head to life and rose to her feet.

Fern pulled the compass from her pocket and

checked for the easterly direction. A mere twenty feet into the dense forest on the far side, she spotted a bright blue tarpaulin hanging from a tree branch. A sun carved into the tree trunk smiled at her. Simon would have been able to reach the makeshift pack. But it was beyond her height by many inches. Whatever bulged in its belly, she was going to find out. And if it wasn't something good to eat, Gregory was in for an earful. Again. She snorted. It was becoming a fun game they played.

She yanked the machete free from its scabbard and swung at the rope. Missed. Swung again. There was no way she'd reach it alone. "Everything about this challenge is impossible!" She stretched to her tippy-toes, stabbed the machete into the bottom of the ball of tarpaulin, and ripped. A cascade of items fell around her like strange contents of a survival-themed piñata. A bottle of water conked her on the head. Yes! A chortle escaped her throat. She sank to her knees and pulled the things to her, like a child hoarding toys in preschool. All in all, two large bottles of water, a package of beef jerky, two cans of tuna with peel-off lids, a jar of peanut butter, and a note from Gregory. *Give a man a fish and you feed him for a day. Teach a man to fish and you feed him for a lifetime.* Fern had heard the old saying before, but what did Gregory mean by it out here? They'd already had more minnows than they could stand. And she didn't think the creek held any large fish.

Ripping the bag of jerky open, she inhaled the

tangy aroma of teriyaki. Heavenly. Her mouth watered as she crammed a piece of the chewy meat into her mouth and closed her eyes. It didn't matter that she'd never cared for jerky before. Today, it was the most delicious thing ever to grace her tongue. She chewed slowly, relishing every moment until it dissolved in her mouth.

The water. Simon needed it. How was she going to get everything back across the waterfall? If she had managed to get the tarp down intact and the rope, it would've made a nice satchel. It hung limply above her, deflated, with its ragged edges blowing in a soft breeze. Ugh. She shouldn't have lost her patience. Should've tried harder to get it down. Too late now, though.

She grabbed the machete and hacked at the tarp until a jagged piece the size of her torso floated to the ground. She'd have to leave the rest. And the rope. She wrapped the food items in the piece she'd salvaged, tied it closed with the string on the fire starter, and headed back toward the tree bridge. Would she manage a second crossing without becoming a permanent fixture a hundred feet below?

Chapter 12

Had Fern and Simon made it to the end of their hike yet? Gregory curled his fist and bounced it off his thigh, gazing out the tower's window toward the north. His father's voice droned on and on at the head of the table. Pops paced in front of the projector, lighting his chest in a myriad of colorful pie charts. Statistics that were barely decipherable before he blocked the view and bounced the data off his stomach.

The other men seated around the massive walnut table payed perfect attention to Pops, their gazes never wavering and their eyelids never drooping. They'd be massacred if they did. They all knew it. Gregory snapped his attention to his father's piercing gaze staring directly into his eyes. Had Pops asked him a question? The silent room and nervous clearing of throats around him told Gregory he'd missed something important. He stopped chewing on the pen lid in his mouth. Sweat broke out on his brow. If Pops had to repeat himself in front of all these underlings, Gregory would be dead. He rolled the dice and took a gamble. "No, sir."

Pops's right eyebrow quirked upward. He turned his back to the room and continued his lecture. "Gregory is correct, even though it was a lucky guess. Our company cannot keep operating at the same level of efficiency unless we find a way to cut our costs. There have been some strange expenditures and money allocations of late. I will discover the truth." Again, Pops drilled him with a stony glare.

Gregory's heart nearly stopped. Did he know that Gregory had deceived him? How? He'd been careful to cover his tracks. No one in the building knew they were filming. Gregory sucked a breath through his teeth. The secretary who'd helped with auditions. Had she talked? He should've fired her before Pops returned from this last trip. Her shifty gaze when she had signed the nondisclosure should've alerted him to her inability to keep her mouth shut. A knot formed in the pit of his stomach. He had to escape before Pops had time to pen him in and question him. He wouldn't be able to lie much longer.

Gregory darted toward the door amid the crowd of men fleeing the harsh meeting. If he kept his head low and shimmied away while Pops had his back to the room, he'd be in his car and gone before anyone noticed.

"Son!"

He froze in the doorway and his shoulders drooped. He hadn't been fast enough.

Watching Fern inchworm her way back across the precarious log made Simon squirm. She'd been right to make him stay, but he didn't like it. He couldn't protect her standing on the sidelines. *Lord, please get her over here.* He patted a sporadic rhythm on his elbow with his opposite thumb. Come on, Fern.

What was it she held between her teeth? Each of her movements out on the log suspended in space made his heart pound harder. Almost there. Just a little farther. Come on, girl. Bring that beautiful face back to me.

Finally, Fern sat on the end closest to them. He could see the shaking of her muscles from where he stood and a thin trail of blood dried on her forearm. He squeezed between the cameramen and offered his hand.

She paused, chest heaving, and handed him the package dangling from her teeth. "Thanks. That was getting heavy."

Simon sat the tarp ball behind him and reached for her waist. He tucked his hands into the depressions above her hip bones. For a moment, they paused eye to eye, and something electric passed between them. He felt it in his toenails. In every fiber of his being. Fern's eyes dilated, her eyelids heavy. She felt it too. No doubt about it.

Someone shuffled their feet and a rock went sailing over the side of the bluff. Fern smiled and ducked her head. He helped her slide to her feet. Once she was on solid ground, he caught her to his chest and wrapped his arms around her. "That was torture." He frowned. He hadn't meant to say that out loud.

Fern jerked and pulled away. "Wanna eat?"

Did he ever. "There really was food?"

"Yep."

"I figured it'd be another trick or clue or test."

Fern held out a slip of paper. "There is a message. But food too." She picked up the tarp and produced a bottle of water. "Water first. I bet you're still a bit lightheaded. Drink."

"Yes, ma'am." He wouldn't argue her tone. Not this time. It was starting to grow on him, the way she took charge. And he was dying of thirst. It didn't take him long to drain the bottle. "I bet we can think of something to use this for. Don't you think?"

"Probably. But not right now. My brain's way too exhausted."

Simon glanced at the sky. With the heavy cloud cover, they only had about an hour of good light left. "We'd better set up temporary camp, eh?"

Fern nodded.

"What happened over there?"

"I found a tarp suspended from a rope in a tree. I couldn't reach the rope, so I had to cut the tarp to get the goodies."

If he'd been there, he could've helped. Probably could've reached it since he was at least a head taller than she. He shouldn't have stayed behind like a useless lump. Fat raindrops began to plop through the foliage, making perfect circles in the dusty earth around them. "Great."

Fern's eyebrows creased together.

"The tarp would've been helpful right about now." He gritted his teeth. Was he really mad at her? Or himself?

"Well, excuse me. I suppose I could've let you try to cross and kill yourself."

"Maybe you should have." Wait. That's not what he meant. "Not the kill myself part. You know what I mean. I could've gotten the whole tarp, and we would be sleeping dry tonight."

Red flared to Fern's cheeks. He'd crossed a line. He knew it. It wasn't her fault he'd had to stay behind. Or that she was too short to reach. If he'd gone, he probably would've done just that. Fallen to his death.

If she weren't so cute when she was angry. A smile played at the corners of his lips.

"What? You think this is funny? I risked my neck to help us. And you don't even say thank you!"

She spun away from him, but he caught her wrist. "Fern, wait. I'm sorry."

"Don't." She yanked free and disappeared into the thick sheet of rain now blanketing the forest.

>>>——▶

Insufferable. That's what Simon was. Absolutely insufferable. She'd risked her life to get them some food, and he had the nerve to complain about her not being able to bring back a tarp? Fern kicked a tiny white pine sapling. Water droplets like clear beads sprayed from the pine's heavy little limbs. For a moment, they sprung back to life, only to be weighed down again by the deluge of raindrops falling. There wasn't a dry spot on her. Yes, the tarp would've been nice. But, if anyone was going to complain about not getting it, it should be her. Not Simon.

She slammed her arms across her chest and sighed. Why was he so aggravating? So intoxicating. The cool rain worked to temper her anger. Fern's eyes unglazed and she attempted to gain her bearings. How far had she walked?

Oh, great. Her hands trembled as she scanned the forest. She didn't recognize anything. Couldn't see Simon or the camera crew. What was she thinking storming off like that? She spied a hemlock with swooping boughs nearby. It wouldn't dry her off, but maybe she could find a little shelter. Fern crawled under the branches and settled her back against the trunk. At least under the protective limbs, she could wipe her eyes and not have them immediately refurnished with fresh raindrops.

Why was she doing this to herself? Was half a million dollars worth this torture? She hugged her knees, dropped her head between her arms, and shivered. Nothing could be worth this. Not even her dream of owning a veterinary hospital? Not even Simon? She sighed again. Why couldn't her stubborn mind stop thinking of everything in terms of her handsome partner?

It was odd to think the world still turned outside their forest home. People were out there somewhere working normal desk jobs. Driving cars. Using microwaves to heat up their pizzas and burritos. Completely unaware that two people were struggling for life in the Tennessee wilderness. There was an entire world of other ways to obtain her dreams. Why suffer any longer?

As soon as the rain let up, Fern would break the news to Simon. She was out of here. Sorry, Simon. He couldn't stand her anyway. He'd probably be relieved to be rid of her, and that she would be the one to give up, not injuring his masculine pride.

What would she do after this though? How could she ever return to normal life as if nothing had happened? As if she'd never met Simon or felt the plunge of electricity surge through her with his touch. If she walked away, would the fact that she could've finished haunt her for the rest of her life? Knowing her, yes. Once she'd had a hearty meal and a hot shower, she'd start replaying every moment out here. Wondering what she could have done differently. Wondering if she could have made it had she been a little tougher.

Wondering what would have become of Simon

and his broad chest and that scruffy beard of his.

The rain slowed to a tinkling pace, soothing with its leaf-drop music. Fern raised her head, wiped her eyes free of rain and tears, and crawled out from under her tree. Which way back to Simon? She felt a slow warmth creeping over her back and hoped it was him. Spinning in her squishy hiking boots, she discovered a shaft of sunlight from the western sky. One singular beam piercing through the thick clouds and forest canopy to land squarely on her. She closed her eyes and soaked in the sunny glow. It filled her chest with a honey-warm bubble that spread internally to her limbs, carried by her slow pulse.

She couldn't walk away from Simon. Not now.

Maybe not ever.

Her eyes snapped open. Maybe not ever? Did she really feel that way?

"Fern!"

She jumped at the sound of Simon's call, straightened her shoulders, and turned in his direction.

He bounded up the hill toward her, a smile plastered on his bluish lips. "I was worried about you. Are you all right?"

Yes. No. She shrugged her shoulders. She'd almost forgotten she was mad at him. "I'm fine." She pressed her lips together. "We'd better set up camp."

"Look, Fern. I'm sorry. The tarp isn't important." He took a step closer.

The intensity streaming from his gaze thawed the remaining coolness all the way down to her toes.

"I'm glad you're okay. I wish I could've helped you. I almost had a heart attack when you slipped."

Droplets of rain clung to his beard. She longed to brush them free. Her heartbeat betrayed her, pounding with the thrill of his nearness instead of the anger it should have been racing from. She cleared her throat and dropped her gaze. "Right. Where are the cameramen?"

"Funny, don't you think, Gregory?"

Gregory knew from the too-cool tone in his father's voice, he didn't find the situation funny at all. "Yes, sir."

"These unaccounted for transfers of funds really have me baffled."

Gregory's gaze hopped from the vase of dead flowers on the table to the evening skyline burning red through the window to the projector, now lifeless after the tense meeting. Anywhere but his father's gray eyes. "Yes, sir."

"That wasn't a question, Gregory."

"No, sir."

"Well, I suppose it is getting rather late. We can discuss this in the morning."

When had his father ever let business wait until morning? That couldn't be a good sign. Maybe his father wanted him to squirm all night long knowing Pops had deduced the truth. Until Gregory came crawling in to confess in the morning. Like when he was twelve and stole the autographed football from the lobby at his father's first firm. Gregory had been unable to sleep all night knowing his father suspected him. Waiting for dawn had been excruciating. He'd been grounded for a month and had to repay every penny of the football's worth before his father would allow him to keep a cent of his own profits from chores. It took a year. How much longer would he be held accountable for this current mess of his?

He sensed a steely, questioning gaze being lobbed his way, but Gregory couldn't meet it. One glance at his father's face was enough to make him scamper from the room. There wouldn't be a conversation in the morning. Gregory wasn't coming back.

Fern excused herself from their temporary camp feigning needing to find a tree. Truth was she needed some space. The weight of the day's events had come crashing into her exhausted mind. She needed someone to talk to, but the men available wouldn't do. She needed Sylvia and a gallon of milk and some peanut butter cookies. Did Max and her little fluff ball, Shintu, miss her? Probably not. Sylvia would be spoiling them rotten with extra treats and belly rubs. Fern's cats probably still hadn't even noticed she was gone. How about Dexter? Would he remember the crazy lady in the woods when he was grown?

She plopped onto a log, broke a brittle branch, and began to peel the bark off in long strips. She could talk to the camera, but then all her intimate thoughts would be fair game for national television. Flipping open the side screen, she threw caution to the wind and pressed record.

"Hey out there. Hope you're enjoying our pain and suffering. It sure makes for good TV while you're on your cushy couches stuffing your faces with popcorn. Right?

"How'd you like that near-death slip earlier? It sure got my heart racing." Kind of like Simon's touch. Her fake smile fell. "You know what? Here's the truth. None of this is easy. None of it is like I expected. I thought I'd waltz out here and flourish. Instead I'm bleeding and bruised, starving and thirsty all the time, wishy washy on my emotions where I've been rock solid since I was a kid. There. Happy, Gregory? I've been broken.

"The things that are keeping me going are a dream of owning my own practice and being able to help people who can't afford care, and Simon. That's it. If it weren't for those two incredibly annoying, aggravating things, I could be home in my bed curled up with my critters eating doughnuts and pizza." Her stomach growled, punctuating her thought. "Why do I have to be so stubborn? I have no idea. But I've come to accept it's as big a part of me as these stick-straight locks of mine." Her stubbornness had gotten her through more than a few rough times. She couldn't regret it being part of her DNA. Scott. College. Vet school.

She nodded. Her gumption would get her through this too. Through all of it, even the ricocheting of her heart in her chest whenever Simon cast his soulful glance her way.

"You did it, Greg. Fern admitted she's broken."

Flying up the interstate, Gregory lifted a fist toward the ceiling. Yes! "That's good news, Turner, my man. Good news. I'll be there in an hour. Call me if anything else happens."

Wouldn't Jenny be proud? Why were his thoughts revisiting his past so much lately? If only he had chosen her over his father's greed back in college, maybe he could have held onto her. Was it because he had no one to share his successes with? His parents wouldn't celebrate, or even view his new venture as a success. His friends, besides Turner, who hated him right now, drifted away after college. Humph. Truth be told, they were drifting before graduation. As soon as he had accepted his fate as his dad's underling, future heir to the family business, all of the "normal" people left him. Like panicked termites abandoning their nest under the intent gaze of a monkey. He supposed he was rather like a foolish monkey, letting his father's dreams influence him as they had for the last decade and a half. He had enough. No more.

He was his own man. For the first time, and he had no one to celebrate with.

Chapter 13

"Ready to go?" Fern paced a few feet away, arms crossed over her chest.

How would he hide the dizziness from her this morning? As soon as they started hiking, she was sure to notice if his steps didn't line up. His head throbbed. Each heartbeat sent a spark of light through the corners of his vision, like fireworks in his retinas. He faked a smile. "Lead the way."

He waited until she turned to rise to his feet. Swayed a bit. Tested his footing and found it to be firm. He wouldn't pass a sobriety test, but maybe Fern wouldn't notice, seeing as how she still seemed angry with him and refused to look back.

The camera crew trudged along with them, seeming much less enthusiastic after the wet, uncomfortable night. Were they worried about their return to base camp and what awaited them there? He would be. Gregory didn't seem the type to push too far. Already he'd made it abundantly clear he expected everyone involved to obey all rules.

This particular task had been as difficult as all the others. How far could they push their bodies before they started to shut down? He sniggered. What was he talking about? His body was well into the process. He lifted his arm and wiggled the flab underneath. That had definitely not been there three weeks ago. Nor had this horrible headache and dizziness. Self-cannibalization. That's what he'd heard the body's natural process of breaking down muscle tissue for energy in times of extreme malnourishment called. Sounded lovely.

Gregory had to know he was testing the limits. What if he really did have more sinister plans for them? The camera crew's whispers in the dark last night were cause to worry. Clearly they believed Gregory was out for blood. Simon frowned. No. It couldn't be true. Too many people were involved for Gregory to be plotting murder. It would be foolish. Unless he didn't care if he was caught. He'd heard serial killers often played games because deep down they wished to be stopped . . .

His toe caught on a rock. He grunted but managed to right himself before Fern turned. She raised her eyebrow and pressed her lips together. He forced a half-smile. Just a little farther and they'd be home. Home? He chuckled. Their camp consisted of a few sticks tied together with honeysuckle vines, a rock fire circle, and dirt. Yet, he longed to get back to it. Though, at least out in the boonies, he wasn't stuffed into his confined little shelter. He'd swear it felt smaller each night, even though is body was shrinking and he should be taking up less surface area. And they had not had that creepy-crawly feeling of being watched that they'd been experiencing at camp. Was it the myriad of cameras eliciting the spine-tingling? Or was Fern correct in believing someone else was out there with them?

Sweat poured from his brow, stinging his eyes, but he hadn't the energy to wipe them. Fern disappeared over the next rise and for a moment Simon was tempted to plop down and take a nap. The cameraman on his heels cleared his throat. Right, he had to keep moving. Was he going to make it back to camp? Simon forced his leaden feet to keep trudging up the hill, his heavy steps scuffling the earth beneath burning feet. At the top, he spied Fern at the base of the descent already. He forced a deep breath into his heaving chest and stepped off the stair-like rock.

His ankle rolled and the knee followed. Darting to the right when it should be aimed forward. His reaction to the tearing pain slicing through the backside of his knee was delayed, like the blood sludging through his veins couldn't carry the messages any faster. With the second wave of pain careening through his thigh, he screamed. Fell to his backside and cradled his knee with both hands.

Fern ran back to him and dropped to her knee.

"What happened?"

His knee had exploded. At least it felt like it. He gritted his teeth. "Torqued my knee."

She grabbed his left hand and attempted to pull it from his knee.

"I'll be fine. Give me a minute."

"You're not okay." Her voice had taken on the tone he'd come to think of as her mothering voice. Irritating when his actual mother used it. But somehow comforting and belly-warming when Fern did. "Let me see."

He shook his head. As long as he kept his hands pressed against the joint, the pain wouldn't spread.

"Simon, you're acting like a five-year-old. Let me see." She frowned. "Now." Fern peeled his hands off.

Pain throbbed through the soft flesh behind his kneecap. He moaned.

Fern addressed the cameraman beside him. "We need a medic."

Deep-voice whipped out a cell phone and pressed it to his ear, pacing far enough away that Simon couldn't hear the conversation. He returned with eyebrows so crushed together they appeared to be one thick, bushy line. "It'll be awhile. Gregory has to get someone to base camp first and then hike in."

"He doesn't have them on standby there?"

Simon pressed a hand back to his knee. Just one, so Fern wouldn't swat it away. How had they not noticed or thought to check on the presence of a medical team when this all began?

Fern began to tug on his waistband.

"What are you doing?" It was his turn to shove her hand away.

"I need to actually see your leg."

"Roll my pants leg up or cut it off or something." Anything other than removing them and Fern seeing him in his filthy underwear. He was breaking every mom everywhere's number one rule. There was no way to have clean underwear out here.

She did as he instructed, gently moving the fabric up his calf. If it weren't for the excruciating pain, he would have enjoyed her touch. Simon squeezed his eyes shut as she attempted to pass it over his kneecap.

Fern gasped.

That couldn't be a good sign coming from a veterinarian who had seen car-smashed animals. "What? What is it?"

"It's not that bad."

"You're a terrible liar."

Though she tried to be gentle, he knew, each touch of her gingerly probing fingers sent hot needles into his leg. "We need to immobilize it. You," she pointed to deep-voice, "do you have any type of first aid kit, belt, anything?"

He fumbled for a moment, and then removed his belt. "This work?"

"How could Gregory send you out here with no first aid kit? Is he crazy?" Fern's mumbled words found homes in the stark expressions of all three cameramen.

Simon had an inkling they'd like to say yes, but the cameras were still rolling.

"Give me your sweatshirt."

The second crewman complied, untied it from his waist, and forked it over.

Again, Simon's hand was swatted away, followed by pain as his leg moved a few centimeters. He ground his teeth.

"Sorry. Almost done."

When Fern's hands stopped flashing in hasty but gentle movements, he found she'd fashioned a padded, belted splint of sorts. Almost as good as his hands protecting the joint.

"It's gonna be awful getting you back to camp. But we'll have to try."

Her shining eyes gave him courage. Why did she have to be so beautiful? So unaware of her own grace and allure? Her eyes so filled with concern, compassion, fear. For him. He nodded.

Right about now, he'd walk through fire if she asked him to.

"You!"

Gregory nearly stumbled. Being the victim of Fern's accusatory finger was no light matter. Her eyes, wide with worry and anger, and maybe even something else, made him want to shudder.

"You should have had a plan in place for accidents. Ridiculous!"

She paced away from him, turned with soldier-like precision, and returned, bringing her fury right along with her, until he was nose to nose with it and all its glorious power. He'd not seen her so furious. So terrified. He wanted to throw his fist in the air again and shout. It was working. All of it was working. He held his hands out, palms up. "You're absolutely right, Fern. One hundred percent. I am sorry for the gross oversight on my part. I assure you, it will be remedied from this moment forward."

Fern's chest deflated a bit. She glanced out of the corner of her eye to where the medic and search and rescue team examined Simon. He caught the flicker, the subconscious widening of her eyelids.

Yes. No doubt about it now. He hadn't manufactured this accident himself, but if he had, it couldn't have played out better.

Her brow furrowed, further marring the smoothness of her features.

Was she going to cry? "The moment I return to base camp, it will be protocol that a paramedic team and search and rescue team are on standby at every moment. And my personal helicopter will be available to launch should we have," he steepled his fingers, "more serious incidents."

Fern's gaze whipped back to him.

"Now, now, I'm not saying that will happen. But we want to be prepared if it does, don't we?"

She nodded. "Yes. Yes, of course."

He turned to address the team evaluating Simon. "What's the verdict? Ms. Evans, wasn't it?"

The brown haired lady in blue jeans nodded but deferred to the woman on her right. "I'm search and rescue, Mr. Vanderbilt. I'm afraid the medics will have to make this call."

"It doesn't look great, if you want the truth," a short, stocky fellow answered.

Gregory's stomach sank. Simon couldn't leave. Not now. Not yet. "What can be done in the field?"

Once again, Fern's rage was shooting his direction.

He cringed.

Fern aimed her sharp finger at his chest. "Are you saying you want him to stay?"

Gregory took a breath and plastered on his most winning smile. "I think the decision should be left to Simon, but if he quits now," he tossed his gaze to Simon's pain-rimmed eyes, "he loses his chance." At redemption. He mentally sent the words to Simon. "You understand what's at stake, don't you, Simon?"

His contestant, clearly in extreme pain, nodded.

The medic said, "The best we can do out here is offer a knee brace. Without imaging, I think at best it is an extreme sprain or strain. Maybe a meniscal tear. At worst, it could be the ACL."

"If it's his ACL, he needs surgery."

"Yes, thank you, Dr. Strongbow."

Fern's eyes narrowed to slits. "You can't make

him stay."

The two medics and Ms. Evans squirmed.

Gregory stepped closer and towered over Fern. "I'd like a word with Simon. Alone."

Simon could feel Fern's gaze on him though she had planted herself on the other side of the camp. The squint of Gregory's eyes was not unpleasant, but it wasn't the most heartwarming thing he'd ever seen either. Fern's was much more appealing.

"Listen, Simon, I'm not sure how you want to proceed. But you and I both know you are here for more than the money."

How did Gregory know exactly what to say to dig his talons in deeper?

"Do you feel like you've done major damage to your knee?"

"It only hurts if I move it."

Gregory chuckled. "Spoken like a real champ, as they say."

There was a world out there. And everyone in it thought of him as a criminal. Why should he go back? Nothing waited for him but more whispers and stares. More dead-end jobs. He cut his gaze to Fern. At least out here, she was with him. He dropped his voice. "I'm not ready to go home."

"Simon, my man." Gregory clapped him on the shoulder. "You won't regret it."

Simon nodded.

"I can't take you to the hospital. Nor can I offer you pain meds. But we do have a brace for your knee. And I won't tell anyone that I slipped you these."

He took the blue capsules marked Advil from Gregory's hand. Too bad there were only two of them. "You know what, keep 'em." No sense in feeling relief if it wouldn't last.

Gregory instructed the medic team to doctor his knee as best they could in the circumstances. The pain was dulling to a steady ache, like a cement block sitting in the joint instead of a tiny little disc. Fern shot arrows from her eyes to everyone who dared look at her, but she returned to his side and didn't budge until the work on his knee was complete. He longed to reach for her delicate fingers. Why couldn't he span the short distance and do it?

Keeping his gaze glued to the arch of her neck, the dip of her collarbone, the curve of her high cheekbone, brought him more comfort than the pain relievers would have offered. His pulse stirred as she bent close to check his pupils again.

"They're still dilated, but they are equal now."

Wait, they weren't equal before? "What does that mean?"

"It means when you fell back there, you scared me half to death."

He grinned. "We're even then."

"Funny. I don't think you fell because of your knee. I think you fell because of your head." She patted his forehead and grinned.

"Oh, so I'm crazy now?"

"Yes." She giggled. "But that's not what I mean. I think when you fell yesterday you had a concussion."

"He fell yesterday?" Gregory's bellow pierced the forest. "Why wasn't it on camera?"

The cameramen, nearly forgotten with the medic team's arrival, now attempted to shrink even farther into the background.

Gregory pointed to the nearest one. "Answer me."

Deep-voice squared his shoulders and nodded.

The breeze paused, surely sensing the tension in the circle and finding greener fields to blow upon. Simon wouldn't have made it through the day prior without the help of the crew. But he knew what was coming before Gregory opened his mouth again.

"You broke the rules. No one has to tell me. You're all fired."

At this point, was that a punishment? Simon saw a grin flash across one of the crew's faces. That man was going home. Away from the chaos and strain. Away from Gregory's unknown motives. Simon almost envied him. But feeling some sense of self-worth was more valuable than any amount of money. At the present moment, this crazy, impossible show was the only way to accomplish that. He smiled at Fern, the care and concern in her eyes stirring warmth in his chest. He wouldn't regret it, even if it did kill him.

Chapter 14

"Do you think Gregory really is trying to kill us?" Fern swatted a mosquito from her cheek. Somehow, she'd either gotten used to their annoying presence or they had decreased in numbers. Maybe she was too exhausted to care as much.

Simon shook his head, a bead of sweat trailing down the crease in front of his ear.

"I guess if he was, he wouldn't have returned this, eh?" She held up the tattered mosquito net. A new one would have been nice, though. Maybe one not full of holes, one that could actually catch a fish.

Simon closed his eyes.

"You hurting?" That was a dumb question. What else could she say? That she hated seeing him like this? That when he fell and she thought he was going home, she wasn't even a tiny bit worried about the money. It was the thought of never seeing him again that had set her heart on jagged edge. How had she gotten to this point? She'd never, ever wanted or believed it would be possible to have this sensation deep in the pit of her abdomen. The one that somersaulted when Simon gazed at her, his eyes open books of pain. If only she knew how to read the script. Wasn't there more to his past than he had confessed?

"I'm sorry, Fern."

She started. "For what?"

"I'm not going to be much use with this." He gestured to the knee brace.

"You weren't much use before." She slid her gaze toward him from the corner of her eyes.

He chuckled. "Touché."

His smile calmed the aching worry gnawing at her gut. "You know what I think?"

"What's that?"

"I think it's about time we started fighting back. Not just trying to survive. You know, digging into the foxhole and waiting out the torture. It's time we started thriving out here." She tossed a can of tuna into the air and caught it, the gentle slap adding authority to her statement. It was time to prove their merit to Gregory. Once and for all. No more getting pushed and shoved around by his impossible clues and scampering about trying to recover. Proactive. That's what they'd be.

Fern peeled the lid off the first of the two tuna cans and inhaled the fishy aroma. "I never thought tuna without mayonnaise and sweet pickles could smell so amazing." She stretched over to allow Simon a sniff.

He nodded stiffly, his mouth remaining the tight, compressed line it had been for hours.

"Want half?"

"I'm not very hungry. Thanks."

She understood that his pain was stealing his appetite, but she wished he would eat. She took a couple bites, using her fingers for a spoon. It was hard to make herself stop, but she had plans for the rest. Using her machete, she cut the thicker, sewn edge from the mosquito net and looped it around to fashion a snare. It wouldn't be one that held very long, but if she listened and ran to the trap as soon as an animal was snagged, maybe she'd get lucky.

"Fern, would you pray for me?"

The machete clanged to the ground and bounced several feet away. "What?"

"Please." Simon squeezed his eyes closed, adjusted his leg using both hands, and exhaled a long, ragged breath.

Her pray? She didn't know how to pray. She didn't even know if she believed that He was truly up there listening. She shook her head. "I can't." As soon as the refusal left her lips, she wished she could bite it back. Couldn't she pretend for Simon's sake? But her parents hadn't raised her that way. To believe in a God who hears His children. Instead, they taught her about a just universe. Good actions brought good results. Bad likewise brought bad. She remembered her mother talking to the trees, plants, sky, animals . . . Everything, as if they were all ruled by unique spirits.

Something uncomfortable yet not unpleasant poked at her heart. "Look, Simon, I . . . I don't know how to pray."

His eyes fluttered open, and he even attempted a half-smile. "It's easy. You talk to the man upstairs."

What if she didn't know if He was there or not?

"Ah, you don't believe in God, do you?"

Had he read her mind? "I don't not believe. It's just my parents didn't raise me talking about God or faith or church or anything."

"It's never too late to learn."

That was probably true, but she couldn't admit she didn't know where to begin. Fern gathered the items and her diary cam. Switching it to night mode, she aimed for the darkness outside and to the south of their camp. Man, she hoped this worked. The goodies Gregory's dare provided them wouldn't last long. She chose a spot several hundred feet from the fire, tied the makeshift snare between two flexible but well established saplings, and laid the can of tuna in the middle of the circle. "Fingers crossed." And toes crossed that they didn't catch Dexter or his mom.

If the little can of fish caught something larger, they could dry it and have a supply for days. She rolled her eyes and slapped her hand to her forehead. Here she was thinking she'd been so clever when all along this had been Gregory's idea. "Give a woman a can of fish and feed her for a day." Great. Another victory for Gregory and his annoyingly intelligent and perceptive mind.

She found Simon dozing when she returned, his deep, regular breaths a testament to how exhausted he must've been. Good. Sleep would mean a break from the pain for at least a bit. The veterinarian in her wanted Simon to seek treatment at a hospital. He needed imaging and possibly even surgery. At the minimum he needed steroids and pain relievers. But she realized during the intense moments while the medics examined him, she wasn't ready to go home. Sure, her body craved rest and real food, but something kept her going. Determination? Fear? Maybe her stubborn streak. Whatever it was, she couldn't shake it off with a simple shoulder shrug.

Was it really the possibility of not seeing Simon that held her in the middle of this remote, terrifying, unforgiving landscape? She wasn't sure she wanted to know.

Her heavy eyelids drifted closed. She would worry about her feelings tomorrow.

Fern awoke with a start and listened for a minute before she moved. Simon's heavy breathing remained unchanged. If it wasn't him snoring, who was it? Chills shimmied up her arms. Was the phantom watching from the shadows again? A sound like Shintu's morning panting when he nudged her cheek to go out for his walk echoed from the direction of the snare trap she'd set. Huff, huff, huff. Silence. Huff-puff. A soft, guttural gurgle. Branches jostled against each other, their rubbing leaves sending a second wave of goosebumps up her back. A stick snapped, closer this time. Heavy footsteps padded across the dirt beyond her line of sight. Pacing. Huff-puff, growl.

"Simon?" Her harsh whisper caused the creature to pause. She nudged Simon's shoulder. "Wake up. I think there's a bear."

Simon's head jerked and his eyes snapped open. "What?" He slurred the word.

"A bear. I think there's a bear."

The animal, still shrouded in darkness, shuffled. Stamped a paw. A sharp clack, clack, clack popped from its direction.

Fern's arm hairs bristled. "Simon, can you get up?" They may have to make a stand. If she was correct, an agitated black bear waited at the periphery of their camp. Ugh, the tuna. No wonder.

She grasped his elbow and helped him to his feet, painful though it was to watch. He'd be better off on his feet if the bear charged into camp. Maybe.

Her trembling betrayed her. Violent dogs, she could handle. Crazy cats, no problem. She'd thought she would be brave enough to handle anything this jungle could throw at her as long as she could protect herself from her partner. How wrong she had been.

A second pop shot at them from the trees.

Her legs threatened to give way. Somehow, she managed to find her shaky voice. "Get on out of here, bear!"

Simon attempted to take a step forward.

Fern caught him around the waist as he fell. His arms flopped over her shoulders, bringing the full weight of his long torso onto her. "Simon?"

"Need to chase it off."

"You're in no shape!"

"Just a little dizzy."

Oh, perfect. "You're burning up." She couldn't hold his weight much longer.

He winced and moaned as she deposited him next to the fire.

She spun and yanked a log from the fire, its end flaring from ember to flame as she lifted it above her head. "Go, bear!"

Instead of the hasty retreating footsteps she'd hoped to hear, suddenly a black snout emerged from the bushes. No, no, no. She backed up five paces, her heart hammering her ribs. She risked a glance at Simon. Not good. His face was pale save for the flushed cheeks and shining sheen of sweat on his brow. She had to do something!

The bear's glowing eyes glared at her, its snout wrinkling as it sniffed the air. It stomped its front paw and clacked its teeth once more.

She shivered. Do something, Fern! The beef jerky. Could the bear smell it through the packaging? If she gave it what it wanted, maybe it would leave. Or maybe it would start to see them as an ongoing food source and visit them again.

It slinked the rest of its massive body from the shadows. And paced as the firelight played in eerie waves on its shiny, black fur. By far, it was the most massive black bear she had ever seen. His glowing, yellow gaze never wavered from hers.

She waved the burning stick toward it, scooped up the beef jerky, and tossed it into the fire. The package melted, curling into itself and releasing a wave of new blue and green flames. The sizzle of the meat hissed through the night air, the smell enticing even to her.

The bear rose onto its hind feet, lifted its huge muzzle, and scented the air.

"Sorry, bear. Go!" Please, just go.

As the jerky burned, a thick smoke rose, turning the aroma from savory to something like burned popcorn. The bear dropped to his feet, threw one last teeth-clack her direction, and retreated into the night.

Fern dropped the stick onto the fire and collapsed next to Simon, burying her face in her hands. Her jaw quivered even as tears squeezed from her tightly-shut eyelids. So much for her brilliant plan.

No, Gregory's brilliant plan. He'd probably laugh if the bear mauled them in their sleep.

She turned her attention to Simon, pressed her wrist to his forehead, and groaned. He needed medical attention. Again.

Simon moaned and tossed his head from side to side as if he were trying to escape. From what, she could only imagine. He wouldn't make it until morning without medicine. She needed some feverwort. She thought she remembered some growing by the creek. Was the bear still out there? Lingering nearby, waiting for the opportunity to steal back into their camp? She couldn't leave Simon and search for a plant in the dark.

But she couldn't wait either.

She cradled her head in her hands, pressing her temples to ward off the coming ache. When she worked at Knox Highway Veterinary Hospital, she was a decisive, in control doctor. What was happening to her? Memories from her years in vet school swarmed behind her closed eyelids. Exhausted nights and early mornings. Espressos to keep a modicum of alertness. They reminded her she'd been indecisive then too. Maybe she was only competent when she was fully rested or hyped up on caffeine. Maybe she was only adequate because of Sylvia's strong presence, guiding hand, and confidence. Why couldn't any of her thoughts seem to make it over a finish line of some sort? If she could lie down and sleep, really sleep, for a couple hours maybe she'd be able to think more clearly. Maybe then she would be able to let her doctor side surface and make a good plan of action for Simon.

But she couldn't wait that long.

Simon moaned again, mumbled something about dark eyes.

In his feverish state, who did he long for to comfort him? Perhaps his mother. Or grandmother. For a moment, she hoped it was her. Simon was different than Scott. By leaps and bounds. She was a different woman now too. Capable of making informed judgments about people and their character. But that didn't mean she had to trust him. Not in the least.

Fern grabbed her camera, switched it to night

vision once more, hit record, and strode toward the creek. "Bear, if you're still out here, you'd better move on." She was in no mood to argue. Simon needed help and she was a doctor for Pete's sake. How could she justify sitting around being all wishy washy when he needed her?

Though the camera helped some, locating the specific plant she sought with its delicate reddish-pink blossoms was not easy. Especially when every five seconds she tossed glances behind her and hoped she didn't meet those yellow eyes again. Finally, she yanked some of the fuzzy leaves free and stuffed them in her pocket. *Please let this work.* Lord? She wanted to pray to Him, but it was almost as hard as finding the feverwort.

She mashed the leaves between two stones, grinding half finely and leaving the other a bit larger. The fine half she dumped into a fresh pot of water. If she gave him too much, he'd have diarrhea, but the right amount, given piping hot should alleviate the fever. She hadn't seen it work since she was a child, but the memory of her father's illness had never left her. Maybe that night was one reason she wanted to be a doctor. Albeit she'd taken an interest in the animal side of things not long after that. Her mother had given her father feverwort that night after his delirium had peaked. Daddy's forehead had burned Fern's fingers when she pressed them to his creased brow. They'd thought he would die that night. Had it been a miracle that saved him? Was she likely to get another one now?

Fern gently removed the wrap from Simon's knee. She'd never seen colors so brilliant on human skin before. Yellow, green, purple, blue, almost the whole rainbow. Including red. That was normal, but the amount of swelling concerned her. Had an infection somehow set up? There hadn't been any lacerations. She bathed the joint and layered the leaf mush at the center of the worst of the bruising.

There was something so intimate about touching Simon's leg while he couldn't protest, couldn't lift a finger to stop her. Couldn't lift a finger against her. He seemed so harmless. Not like she imagined a strong, tall man like him would be. She trailed a finger down the line of his jaw, tempted to sink her fingers into the fluff of his beard and see how deep it was.

The night she and Scott had parked on that lonely, dark road, she hadn't put up enough of a resistance. How had she not seen the truth? Scott never cared for her like she had him. She was a kid infatuated that an older boy, a man, was paying such special attention to her. There was so much more to the story she hadn't told Simon. It pressed on her, suffocating her with the voracity of its magnitude. Its shame. It wasn't simply a skeleton. It was a verdict. She'd done awful, horrible things that God, if He did exist, had surely turned His face from long ago. She'd given her innocence to someone who took advantage of her naivety and then tossed her to the side the moment she needed him.

Would Simon do the same thing? Weren't all men out for only one thing—their own needs and wants?

Fern cupped his chin, buried somewhere under the scruff, and examined the lines of his face. Who had Simon hurt in his lifetime? Was the accident his only secret? The sudden urge to press her lips to his forehead overtook her. There was no harm in it. Simon would never know. As she leaned closer, her lips tingling with anticipation, Simon's eyes fluttered open.

"Fern?"

She jumped, paused, only inches away, and sighed. He was awake. But her relief was short-lived. Simon slipped quickly back into the restless dream world. Fern pulled away, instead lifting his head with one hand and pressing the pot of feverwort tea to his lips. He sputtered but managed to swallow a few large sips. It would have to do until dawn.

"Who are you, Simon Fincuff? Are you worthy of my faith?" As she looked to the star-dipped sky, her voice dropped to a shaky whisper. "What if I trust you and you let me down?"

Chapter 15

Sunrise came in slow waves. First a subtle graying of the horizon, followed by a brilliant spark of red. Orange followed on red's heels until the yellow orb broke free and spewed warmth onto the trees. Fern watched the progression from her perch next to Simon's head. His fever had broken sometime in those dark hours before dawn. Thank goodness. He needed real nutrition, real medicine, and a real doctor. Would Gregory let him leave?

"Want him to feel better?"

Fern nearly jumped out of her own skin. How had Gregory snuck up on her? She spun on him and snapped her finger into position. "You have to take him to a hospital."

"He doesn't want to leave, Fern. He told me himself yesterday."

"He's delusional. You have to take him."

"Look, how about a compromise? I brought the medic team. We have an IV and saline. We will get him patched right up. And you, you can have the next clue. It was meant for both of you today, but I will make an exception to the rules. Just this once."

Hadn't he said "just this once" before? "I'm not interested."

"You should be. The prize at the end of this dare could mean the difference between finishing and giving up." Gregory pointed at Simon. "For him, it could mean the difference between life and death."

Fern's heart dropped. "What are you talking about?"

"Clearly, he needs antibiotics. An infection has set up somewhere. That's why he's been writhing all night."

"Obviously."

"There's a surprise waiting half a mile that way. You have permission to go outside the perimeter today." He pointed east, toward the blazing sun. "In the middle, you'll find what Simon needs."

Gregory's snicker sent chills crawling up Fern's arms.

The medic team squirmed and shuffled their feet.

"How well is he paying you?" Her voice battered their already grim faces. "Can't you even look at me?" The two men from the day before slowly raised their heads. "He's going to kill him and you're going to let it happen? We aren't contestants anymore. We're prisoners!"

"Really, Fern. This is unnecessary." Gregory smiled his most winning smile. "No one is trying to kill anyone. There's help right over the hill. You run along now and bring it back while we get an IV in."

Fern's nostrils flared. Run along now? Like a child chastised by a loving father? Not in his lifetime. She'd "run along now" and be back so quickly his head would spin. As soon as Simon woke up, they'd hike out of this mess and escape. Forget about the prize money. They couldn't spend it, anyway, if they were dead.

She stomped through the forest, past the pink flag markers, and found herself gazing up a tall oak tree at a ropes course spanning the distance between the treetops like a nylon spider web. "No sweat." She rubbed her hands on her pants leg and grabbed the first rope rung. Made it to the little platform waiting at the top without any trouble. How had Gregory had the time to erect all of this? Money could make about anything happen, she figured. At the snap of his well-manicured fingers, people jumped and obeyed.

In a manmade squirrel's nest of sorts, Fern inspected the two channels leading off the platform. One was marked with a spray-painted H, the other with an E. Which one led to "the middle?" She stepped onto the E bridge, gripping the rope side rails with tight fists. It wobbled wildly, but she made it across to the next intersection. Faced with a choice between P and X, she chose P. Fifteen steps later, she met a dead end at a prickly pine tree. X proved the same.

Maybe this would be harder than she thought. She rushed back to the beginning and headed down the H path. She tried not to finish the questions in her mind that wondered how well engineered this treetop maze could be. Instead, she focused on keeping her eyes glued to the end of each bridge. She had to get help for Simon. At the end of H, with the silent forest drumming into her ears, she met a choice between Y and O. What was Gregory trying to spell? If she could figure that out now, she'd save a lot of time with incorrect guesses. Hope? Home? Honor? What started with H-Y? Hype? Her heart pounded even harder. Hypocrite. She closed her eyes and bit back a groan.

The Y path swayed more than the others. Her knuckles turned white as she rocked twenty feet above ground. She had to hurry. Simon needed her. Her wobbling knees argued, but she forced her steps forward. The twists and turns continued, the ground falling farther away as she followed P, O, C, R, I, T and E higher into the trees. At the last turn, another platform waited for her with a set of handlebars head-high. A zip line cable disappeared through the trees at a sharp angle. She'd done this before at Dollywood. What a fun way it had been to spend the day. There were helmets and safety harnesses and carabiners strong enough to hold a person three times her size. And her brother at her side, laughing and making memories.

There was none of that here. Gregory really took that waiver of death form she signed seriously, didn't he? She wiped her hands again and gripped the metal bar. Took a deep breath and sailed into the forest. The wind whooshed over her ears and stole her breath. Don't fall. Don't fall. Tears streamed from the corners of her eyes. Her hands burned, fingers cramped. But she couldn't let go. She couldn't. A stout sycamore tree sped toward her. Its peeling bark looming larger and larger. Fern winced and squeezed her eyes shut. She was going to be a splattered pancake. Nothing left but pieces.

The zip line lurched to a stop. She felt herself flying through the air, curling into a ball, and slamming into the ground. The forest floor pummeled the breath out of her lungs as she rolled and rolled. When she finally stopped, she peeled her eyes open and struggled for air. Oh, that hurt. She rolled onto her side and lay there like an injured pup. How much time passed she couldn't be certain, but ever so slowly life returned to her lungs. She wiggled each peripheral part of her body one at a time and found them unscathed. As she sat up, she gazed back to the tree where the handles still rocked back and forth on their tether. Nailed to the tree was one eleven by fourteen manila envelope.

She struggled to her feet, yanked the envelope down, and tore it open. There was no medicine inside. The liar! She slid a black and white photo free and the cutout of a letter H. A much younger Simon sat in the passenger side of a beat-up truck. A scruffy-looking boy that shared Simon's nose gripped the steering wheel. The date in the corner read May 18, 2005. How was some old red-light camera photo supposed to save Simon?

The paramedic placed an IV as soon as Fern left. Ran a bolus of saline and bolstered it with intravenous antibiotics.

"Mr. Vanderbilt, sir, this man really should be in a hospital."

"Nonsense. You're doing a fine job. I bet a thousand dollars when Simon is alert, he will tell you he wants to stay." He can't go home. Not yet. Gregory had done a satisfying job analyzing Simon. So far, he was right on the money about Simon's mental state. Tough, determined, and on a mission. Not to mention falling in love.

Not fifteen minutes after the cool, flushing fluids rushed Simon's dehydrated body, his eyes fluttered open.

"Hey, welcome back to the land of the living, as they say." Gregory patted Simon's shoulder. "You gave us a bit of a scare there."

Simon opened his mouth but nothing came out other than a pitiful squeak.

"Gentleman, this man needs water. And a good meal."

Gregory reached for the backpack at the medic's feet. He held a bottle so Simon could drink, and then unwrapped a sub sandwich layered with roast beef, cheddar cheese, lettuce, and tomato. Gregory chuckled as Simon's eyes widened. "This will be our little secret, okay?"

Simon shook his head. "Can't . . . Eat . . . Fern."

"Well, no, I would certainly hope not. Cannibalism is rather frowned upon in the modern world, wouldn't you say?" He glanced around but found he was the only one laughing at his joke.

Gregory took in the wrinkled-up expression on Simon's face one more time. He was serious, wasn't he? "Okay, tell you what. You guys have been real champs out here. I will give you half and it's up to you what to do with the other." Simon nodded and reached for the sub, but Gregory pulled it out of reach. "On one condition. You stay. You complete the challenge. And you don't breathe a word of this conversation to Fern." Sometimes he wondered what it would be like if the rest of the world was as good at reading people as he was. They'd be able to tell he was baiting Simon. Challenging his moral fibers and his drive to form a permanent bond with Fern. Gregory fully expected Simon to come clean to Fern at some point. In fact, he was counting on it. So much was riding on the undercurrent of this show. No one could see it but him. Not yet.

"Whaddya say, Simon? Stay or go?"

"Stay."

He knew it. Again. Simon had too much to prove to go home now. "We are going to leave you pain meds, an anti-inflammatory, and oral antibiotics. Your partner is perfectly well suited for a situation such as this. Wouldn't you say?" Gregory didn't wait for Simon's answer. "Just a few days' worth of meds. Wasn't part of my original idea for this show, but, hey, it's everyone's first go at this. Good time to learn and see how far we can get, eh?"

"Are you hungry?"

Simon shaded his eyes with his forearm. "Starved. That sandwich is long gone."

Fern pulled their newest dare from the tips of the drone's plastic feet. "How's the knee doing? Think you're up for a little scavenger hunt?"

He chuckled. "Guess I have to be, eh?"

"Aw, come on. Isn't three days long enough for you to be loafing around while I do all the heavy lifting?" She tossed a grin his direction, but inside she quaked. Three days of watching him in pain, fear for his life constantly hanging on the edge of her thoughts. How could he have made the decision to stay? It was foolish, yet somehow she understood the need to finish this crazy challenge. To prove his worth, his grit. His loyalty.

To her.

The thought warmed her stomach. She hadn't managed to get much good sleep, finding herself staring in the direction of his shelter long into the nights. Sleeping next to him beside the fire didn't seem like such an awful idea now. Why had she insisted on putting so much space between their shelters? Her reasoning seemed so much more plausible and justified all those long weeks ago when they had begun.

"It was so sweet of Gregory to put the challenge on hold for a few days. Hey, you never told me what you found out there while I was incapacitated."

No, she hadn't. She'd hidden the envelope in her shelter and hoped it didn't rain. She knew the photo was significant somehow. Was Simon ready for another of Gregory's painful truths? "There was a letter. H, to be exact." She averted her gaze.

"And?"

She bit her lip. She would have to tell him eventually. Might as well get it over with. "A photo."

He was slow to respond. "Of who?"

"You."

"Show me." He struggled to his feet and extended his hand.

She dug in the leaves at the back of her shelter and returned with the envelope. "I can't figure out what it means. Or why the letter H, unless Gregory really wants to rub in the fact that we are hypocrites."

Simon ripped the envelope and removed the photo. The color blanched from his face. "How many people have seen this?"

His tone made her shrink. "I have no idea."

"You . . . You have to forget you've ever seen it. Okay?" He crumpled the photo and tossed it onto their fire. Green and blue flames shot upward, accusations flying in the smoke.

"Simon, I didn't carry it out here. Remember? Gregory has already seen it."

His trembling shook his now loose-hanging shirt. "It can't be. No one knows. No one can find out."

"Find out what? Knows what?" Simon didn't seem to hear her. The look in his eyes terrified her, and for the first time since they'd met she actually felt afraid of Simon. Even in the days after his confession she never truly felt fearful of him. Irritated, yes. Hiding from her own past, yes. Was there more to the story? Maybe he'd lied before, played down the murder charge to earn her trust. Tightness squeezed her heart. Had he tricked her into caring about him? Into worrying about him when he was sick? "Simon?" Her voice sounded small.

He spun around and looked as if he was noticing her presence for the first time. "I don't want to talk about it. Not now. Not ever." He balled his fists. "I'll go home before I tell."

Heat flared up her neck, licked her cheeks. "Go home? After all you've been through? After everything we've accomplished. We're almost there and you want to go home because of a stupid photo?"

He clamped his lips shut. His jaw muscles bulged. Before she could utter another sound, he spun away and hobbled into the forest beyond their camp. Her filter broke free. "That's it then? You're going to walk away?" She didn't know if he heard her. She didn't care. Her life's motto had been right. When she thought she could place her faith in another human being, he was going to be like all the rest. A disappointment. A mistake. A regret.

Her fury fizzled into unwanted tears. For a moment, she almost let them fall. Though she felt as if she might break, she squared her shoulders. If Simon wanted to be difficult, fine. She'd complete today's challenge alone. She'd done enough of that the past week, anyway.

DARE
Today's challenge is two-fold.
A sport that lays its roots in the old.
Follow the flags northeast until you spy
A yellow flag with a tie.
At its base the tools you need
To garner supplies and clues to lead.

Sheesh, Gregory's cheesy riddles sure could use some help.

She filled an empty water bottle from the pot on the fire, grabbed the compass, and set out in the direction of base camp. The forest looked the same. Same logs. Same leaves. Same pink flags.

Yet, it was so vastly different. What would it feel like to change clothes? Could she remember how to drive a car? Use a cell phone? The world placed utmost importance on everyday items, but she hadn't missed them at all. If she had enough food and a better shelter, she could just about live out here forever. No time constraints. No social media and television clogging her synapses.

Like the homestead.

Her feet paused and she chuckled. Her mother would be tickled to hear these thoughts running through her mind. Oh hey, mom. All it took for me to see the value of the homestead was to be dropped into the middle of nowhere and face down starvation, heights, a crazy television show owner, and a hungry bear. Oh hey, mom, all it took to get me to admit the most painful night of my life was to be faced with a handsome, bearded man and the promise of food.

She shook her head. Simon was going home. And that meant she was too. She wasn't ready to face reality yet. She wasn't ready to face the new person she would invariably see in the mirror. *Please, Simon, stay a little longer. Lord, if you happen to be there, please help him stay.*

A breeze tickled her jaw line, fluttering the stray strands of hair across her eyelids. She took a deep breath and smiled. Was God out there after all? Her first real prayer was refreshing.

The flags led her to a narrow meadow with late-blooming daffodils bursting from its fringes and cameras dotting every available tree. Through the center ran a cord, parallel to the ground, higher than her head by at least three times. Bags that looked like the money pouches on Disney's *Robin Hood* waited, suspended from the rope on short strips. She approached a post with a yellow ribbon tied to it and peeled a Ziploc open to read the rules.

"Use the arrows to shoot the bags free. Each one contains a useful clue and some contain a few supplies. You can keep the bow and arrow only if you manage to drop five bags. Don't lose this one, Simon."

Simon. Humph. She could do this too. It had been a long time since she'd shot a bow, but the targets were so close surely she could manage. She scooped up the quiver and compound bow, notched an arrow, and aimed carefully.

The orange-shafted arrow sailed over the line and into the far reaches of the meadow. Okay, strike one. This one would be better. She let loose a second arrow. It followed much the same arc as its companion.

Why couldn't she do this? As she set the third arrow into place, she noticed the shaking of her slim hands. They, like her arms, were surely someone else's. She felt her side. Each rib protruded. Her hip bones jutted from flabby skin. How much weight had she lost out here? As if on cue, her stomach grumbled. "Yeah, yeah, I hear you."

She took a steadying breath and took aim. The arrow fell short and stabbed into the ground, its shaft quivering with the force of impact. "Oh, come on!"

"Need some help?" Simon emerged from the tree line.

She pouted. "No."

"Okay. I'll sit and watch then. You can do this."

Having an audience was worse than accepting his help. But she was still upset with him, wasn't she? Most of the fire washed away with her sweaty hike. All she wanted now was something to eat. "Aren't you going home?"

He shook his head.

Her heart soared to the tips of the trees. He wasn't giving up on them. On her. "Here, you try then." She pointed at the bags. "Get them down and we keep whatever's inside and the bow and arrows."

"This is even better than the one I brought. Do you know what kind of meal we could get with this beauty?"

His infectious smile broadened her lips. Meat. Lovely sizzling meat over their fire. "Squirrels?" she teased.

"For you, I'd try."

Heat flushed her abdomen. He shot her one last grin that made even her toes squirm, and then took aim and fired at the middle bag. The arrow thudded into its burlap side, and the bag dropped like a stone to the grass.

"You did it!"

"Did you doubt me?"

She giggled. "Never, kind sir."

Simon released the rest of the arrows and dropped six more bags. Fern's fingers itched to discover the contents inside. She scooped up the first bag and untied it to find it full of sand. Her shoulders drooped. Dumping it on the ground, she found a cut-out letter D. She carefully ran her fingers through the pile but found nothing else of merit. The next bag contained smooth creek stones and the letter T. The third had a bottle of water and an E. DETH? What in the world did that mean? Add an A and she'd have . . . A chill swept up her body.

"What've you got?" Simon asked.

"Letters. You?"

"A pocketknife, a flashlight, and a protein bar. No letters."

"No fair. You got all the good ones."

He extended his hand and helped her to her feet. She wobbled. He pulled her against his chest.

"You okay?"

"Mmm-hmmm." Soaking up the goodness of the surprise embrace.

"We're a team, Fern. I'm sorry I thought about leaving. And we share the supplies. Like we've done the whole time."

Except for her machete. Was she ready to release the power having it on her side every minute allowed her? She burrowed her face deeper into his chest.

"I know what the photo means," he whispered. "I can't tell you right now, but I promise I will."

She hadn't ever put much stock in promises. But for the first time in her life, she almost believed in this one.

Chapter 16

The trip back to camp started well enough. The pain in his knee had declined rapidly with the medicines Gregory and his team had provided. The brace made walking downhill and over the bumps and lumps on the forest floor challenging, to say the least. But the sky was clear and, for once, the sun didn't seem to be a blasting furnace. He had grown quite comfortable with himself as a wild man. And the company was stupendous. He smiled and glanced over his shoulder. Fern followed, having insisted he lead so he could set the pace.

He wanted so badly to tell her the truth. He swallowed hard and stopped. Her warm hand instantly on his shoulder soothed him. He motioned for her to cut the feed on her GoPro camera and he did the same. "Do you see any other cameras?"

Fern glanced at the nearby trees and shook her head. Her forehead wrinkled. "Are you okay?"

He shook his head. "I want you to know what

really happened the night of the accident. But it can't be part of this show. I may have to lie in order to convince Gregory to give us the next clue, but I don't want to lie to you. Promise me this will stay between us?"

Fern nodded in time to the thudding of his heart. He licked his lips and released a cleansing breath. "I wasn't the one driving that night."

Fern sucked in a breath through her parted lips.

"I took the fall to protect my brother, Lance."

"You went to jail for someone else's crime?"

"I love him. I couldn't let him pay for my stupidity. You see, it was my idea to go to that party. To get so wasted I couldn't drive. I thought he was sober. But I guess I was so drunk I couldn't tell he had been drinking too."

"Oh, Simon." She placed her hand on his forearm, sending warmth coursing through him.

"I could handle prison. Lance couldn't. He's not as tough." Simon sighed. "But he is paying for that night nonetheless. Instead of moving on like I hoped he would, he is drowning his past in the bottle. When I got out and came home, I thought I'd see the happy young boy I'd left. He wasn't there anymore. And I don't know how to help him." A knot burst like an aneurysm in his chest. Releasing years' worth of worry, guilt, and anxiety. He drew a ragged breath and risked a glance into Fern's eyes.

She smiled with wide eyes. "You can't shoulder his burdens for him."

Coming from anyone else, Fern's statement probably would have raised the urge to argue. "No, I suppose not. I wish I could. I threw my life away trying. Do you know how long it has been since someone looked at me with anything but scorn? I've been branded a criminal. A murderer."

"You and God know the truth. And now me."

"Sometimes that's not enough, you know? I want things to go back to the way they were before. My whole future ahead of me, dreams of a career in football and a family after college. I'll never have any of that." He chuckled. "I can't even keep a job, though I work as hard as any man. The stigma is enough to label me an outcast."

"I'm sorry. If it helps, I don't even notice the jailbird stamp on your forehead anymore."

When he felt so near to tears, his laugh surprised him. He rubbed his forehead, knowing Fern was joking but on some level feeling like the people in the Bible branded in the book of Revelation.

Fern stopped his fingers and took them in her hand. "Why are you out here, Simon?"

He found courage in the soft wells of her dark eyes. "Redemption. A chance to start over."

"Me too."

His eyebrows shot up. "What have you got to be redeemed from?"

Her eyes darkened. "I'm not ready to tell you yet. I hope you can understand that."

He longed for her to trust him, but he understood

why she couldn't. For now, it was enough to claim her hand in his and feel the tingling her touch gave him. He nodded. "What do we tell Gregory?"

"Oh, right. Switch your camera back on. We'll think of something."

"Wait." He wrapped his arms around her shoulders and hugged her, planting a kiss on the top of her head. "Thank you for not judging me."

"I have no room to judge." She paused and when she spoke her voice sounded so tiny. "I prayed earlier."

"You did?" He pulled back and smiled. "I'm proud of you."

"I don't know much about God, but I think I'm finally ready to learn."

He knew his smile radiated joy down on her. He gazed at her lips, the color of Ambrosia apples. He'd be willing to bet they were as sweet. By the skin of his teeth, he managed to refrain from finding out. The time wasn't right. If he was lucky, maybe it would be soon.

They flipped their cameras on, and he held his breath hoping Gregory wouldn't notice the difference in time stamps on the feed. He needed to think up a story to convince Gregory of a non-truth realistic enough to sound like it.

The unyielding knee brace soon set his thigh and calf to aching. He halted at a fallen maple and plopped stiff-legged onto its worn surface. The bark had long since sloughed off. No doubt its streaked, holey surface was filled with grubs. But no matter how his stomach rumbled, after the earthworm stew, he couldn't seem to work up the courage to suggest they look for some. Hopefully, Dexter was fattening his tiny little body on them out there somewhere. Simon was happy to let the critter hog them all.

The log rolled slightly as Fern took a seat a little farther away. The rustle of something creeping amid the leaves reached his ears. It sounded almost like someone squishing a plastic shopping bag. Or gently folding aluminum foil. He leaned forward and, directly between his wide-spread feet, a pointy, scaled tail attempted to work its way into hiding. Or was it trying to attract his attention? The color of a Yellow Green Crayon, it wriggled like a slow worm.

"Fern?" He pointed at the strange, writhing tail.

Her eyes widened and her nostrils flared. "Don't move, Simon. Not even an inch."

"Why? What is it?"

"Copperhead."

Was she teasing him? He scoffed. "They're not yellow."

"Juvenile. The tails can be yellow-tipped. It helps them attract prey."

His smile faded. "You're kidding, right?"

"I'm dead serious."

So, with his bum knee making him slow as a slug, he was sitting directly over a venomous snake's head, somewhere directly below an area he'd rather not imagine being bitten? Wonderful. He froze, afraid to even blink for fear of disturbing their slithering friend.

"I'm going to look for its head. If I say, 'Jump,'

be ready to get out of the way. Okay?"

He shook his head and dipped his chin toward his knee.

"It'll be fine. Just stay calm."

Fern paced back ten feet or so directly in front of him and squatted down. She shielded her eyes and pressed her lips to a thin line.

He was riveted by her intense gaze, refusing to let his thoughts continue down the path they were taking worrying about what soft, fleshy part of him the fangs would land. "Too bad we can't eat him."

For a moment, Fern started to smile. "I can't see the head, but he would be delicious."

Simon risked a glance between his legs. He was met by two narrow-slitted eyes that made him shiver. A large angular head and large venom pouches for such a short-appearing snake.

It flicked its tongue slowly forward, no doubt tasting Simon and Fern on the air.

He moved slowly toward an erect position, but, even though his movements were slight, the snake instinctively coiled into the characteristic S-shape that meant defense was imminent. "Um, Fern?"

"Don't move." From the top of his field of vision, Fern disappeared from his view. Moments later, she was beside him pressing the machete into his open palm. "I am going to try to get his attention fixed behind the log. Take a deep breath and aim for his head. Not a time for hesitating."

Simon couldn't even whisper his agreement with

his throat as tight and dry as it had ever been. *Lord, please help! I don't want to die this way.* He heard a thud on the log behind him. For an instant, the shortest one in his life, the snake's posture turned. Just slightly. But enough to give Simon the courage to plunge the machete into the recess between his feet. He held the weapon tightly against its sinking point and hoped he'd hit the target. When nothing appeared to bite him and the tail became still, he released the machete and took a staggering step forward. Somehow, Fern was there to catch him, her small but strong hands on his chest pushing him to a stop.

"I think you got it. You can stop running now."

He closed his eyes and sighed. Soaked in the feeling of her hands on him, grounding him. "I wasn't running away."

She laughed. "Right."

"Hey, I got dinner. Don't make fun of the big, brave hunter." He faked a pout. "Come on, let's get back to camp before it spoils."

"I can already hear the meat sizzling."

Fern fully expected to find Gregory waiting for them in camp. Though how he would manage to pass them and get there first, she wasn't sure. The man was like a magician. Always one step ahead of them. Always seeming to read her thoughts. Knowing things about their past no one else knew. Did he know that part of her past too?

As the evening waned, and Gregory didn't materialize, her unease only grew. With a full belly for the first time in days, she longed to lie beside the crackling fire and rest. Instead, she paced back and forth. Back and forth. "Why do you think he hasn't come yet? He seems to know everything. There's no way he missed our time out."

"Come sit down, Fern. You've asked me the same question a hundred times."

She nodded, but her pacing didn't slow. Her stomach stirred in restless waves. If Gregory managed to get ahold of that photo and suspected the truth of Simon's past, how much more about her did Gregory already know? Was it her turn for another truth next? One she'd vowed to never speak of again? Her heart clenched. She couldn't speak those words out loud. Admit to what she'd done. Not to anyone, and especially not on camera where everyone in the United States would be free to judge her. To condemn her. To hate her for the awful person she really was.

"Come sit, Fern. You need to rest."

"I can't!"

"This is about more than today, isn't it?"

She nodded once and wrung her hands together.

"It seems we both have more secrets. You can tell me. Anything."

Her throat ached. "No." She backed away from him. She wanted to run. Disappear into the forest. Never face the past. "I can't."

He faced both palms her direction. "Easy, Fern. It's okay. Everything's okay."

Simon was right. Her secret was still safe. Gregory couldn't force her to do anything. If all else failed, they could come up with a story like with Simon's newest revelation. It would be fine. Her breathing slowed. "Okay. Everything's okay." Her attention snapped to Simon's worry-drawn face. "Do you think Gregory will be here in the morning?"

"I'd about guarantee it."

"You ready?" She didn't have to specify, they both knew what she meant.

He flattened his lips and nodded.

This was good stuff. Great stuff, actually. Gregory leaned back into his swivel chair, set the bottle of formula on the desk, and tucked his hands behind his head. "She's a worried mess, Turner. Are you seeing this?"

"Hard to miss, boss."

Turner had taken to calling him boss the last few days. Not Gregory. Not friend. Not buddy. Boss. Gregory hadn't meant to alienate his only remaining friend, but how could he explain everything? It was better to show him. Gregory could mend the fences, as they say, when the show was over and everything was out in the open.

"Keep this fur ball in here," Turner said. "I'm

going to take a break."

Gregory snapped his fingers, and the little raccoon came running. He certainly had grown over the last days, doubling his size. And his curiosity. He snatched him from the floor and scratched behind the little guy's ear, a favorite location if Gregory were to judge by Dexter's gentle purring. The kit slipped off to sleep as Turner slipped through the canvas and zipped the door behind him.

"It's almost time to take you back to the woods, little fella."

Dexter didn't seem to hear him, lost in a dream, it seemed, with his front paw twitching like a pup's.

Next year, they would have cabins with real roofs and electricity. And nicer bathrooms than the Port-a-Johns he'd rented. Next year, he would have a fan base and some credibility and could push even harder.

He grinned as Fern resumed her pacing on the monitor. He should have zipped down to camp like she suspected, but something told him to hang back. Meanness? Possibly. Letting her sweat all night would make for more explosive reactions tomorrow. But it was time to let his little birdies fly on their own and see what happened. More time to stew probably meant more time to corroborate their stories. More time to bond. He could antagonize them in the morning.

Chapter 17

Morning sun rode in waves across Fern's eyelids. Yellow, red, gray as the trees rustled under a gentle breeze. Fifteen days out here felt like home. Their camp. Their fire. Their place in the wilderness carved by beads of sweat and stubbornness.

She wasn't ready to go home. It didn't matter much that she missed her pets. She would miss this place even more. The way the leaves waved hello each morning. The way the sunset saluted goodnight each evening through a painting of dark-trunked trees.

The way Simon looked at her, as if she were precious. Something to be honored. She'd never been looked at like that before. Her smile fell. He wouldn't feel that way once he knew about the decision she'd made at the ripe old age of sixteen. Especially since she knew the truth about his chivalrous self-sacrifice. He wasn't a murderer at all. He was a hero.

"Good morning, campers."

Gregory's voice ringing out from the forest made Fern scamper from her shelter. Simon already stood at attention nearby.

Gregory approached. He waved a finger and tisk, tisked. "You broke the rules again, Simon."

Simon's jaw muscles bulged. For once, Fern had no retort.

"I'm getting really tired of this game." He chuckled at his pun.

Fern rolled her eyes. "You know what? I'm calling your bluff. You've invested too much to send us home over something like a blip in the film feed."

Gregory's face turned red. "A blip? Is that the story you're really going to tell me?"

She squared her shoulders and opened her mouth to fire hot words, but stopped when Simon stepped forward, looming over Gregory.

"It's fine, Fern." His gaze never broke contact with Gregory's. "You want to know what was said and done during our time off-camera, right?"

Gregory nodded.

"I told Fern the truth about that photo."

"You'll not get another clue until you—"

"Tell the truth. I understand. We know how this works by now, Mr. Vanderbilt."

"Out with it then."

"My brother and I were both so drunk, the details are a bit fuzzy. But, at some point, as gross as it sounds, I needed Lance to pull over so I could . . . You know . . . Get sick. I took over driving and not a mile down the road we had the accident. It's as simple as that."

Fern held her breath. Did Gregory already know the actual truth?

The two men, toe-to-toe, eyed each other for many long moments. Like bucks sizing each other up before a fight. Gregory's shoulders slumped. Was he disappointed by Simon's story? Maybe he was hoping for a more shocking revelation.

"Very well, then." He fished in his shirt pocket. "Here is the next clue, Fern."

Her heart skipped a beat. Not a truth one for her. Please.

She took the note from Gregory and waited until he walked away to unfold it.

DARE

Fern released the breath she'd been holding. A dare was far better than a truth at this moment.

"*Inscribed upon the wall*
Are more letters you will need.
Clues to bring you closer to the prize
And clues to make your head reel.
Within this challenge,
You will find the next.
Above the fall, dangle, don't dream.
Cryptic as usual. Not quite as cheesy, though."

Simon looped his arm around her shoulder and leaned closer to get a better view of the poem. "Think he means our waterfall?"

The feel of his well-muscled arm around her shoulders knocked her senses out of whack. All she could think as she turned her head was how his strong profile seemed more handsome than ever. His breath, warm on her neck, stole hers. He lifted his head and gazed into her eyes, sending her pulse bounding away like a frightened antelope. Suddenly self-conscious, she swiped at a mosquito on his nose, breaking the intensity of the moment.

"We'd better get started." The husky tone in his voice sent ants crawling down her spine.

Was he affected by her nearness like his moved her? "Right. Yes." She jumped to her feet, flinging Simon's arm from her shoulders. "I'll run down and check the waterfall, and if I find anything I'll come back and get you. No sense in you hiking down with that contraption on your leg if there isn't a need to."

At Simon's hesitant nod, Fern rounded the corner, passed the clump of honeysuckles drowning their fellow ground-dwelling weeds, and arrived creek-side in a matter of minutes. A cloud passed over the sun and paused its sky-flight, casting a dark shadow over the creek. The hairs on the back of her neck stood on end. The same queasy feeling in the pit of her stomach told her without a shadow of a doubt someone, or something, was watching her. Had the bear returned? Had Gregory decided to hang back? "I . . . I know you're out there. Show yourself!" Nothing moved. Not even a breath of wind. "Hello? Come out!" She placed her left foot forward, coming to rest gently on the ball. Still nothing moved. No crackling leaves or popping sticks. But the feeling that someone's gaze was glued to her every move would not be shaken.

A rustle echoed from the undergrowth behind her. She spun on her heels as a gray blur dashed from the mass of honeysuckle vines up the hill. Fern blew out a sharp breath and brought her hand to her chest. Underneath, her heart pounded. "Dexter?" The raccoon halted, rose onto his back feet, and cocked his head sideways as if to say he was listening. "You scared me, you little rascal." She expelled a nervous, shaky laugh and squatted. "You've gotten big."

Dexter dropped to all fours and took an unsure step in her direction.

She snapped her fingers gently and cooed soft reassurances. "I'm glad to see you're okay." She would love to fondle his soft ears once more. To feel the bristly-smooth fibers of his tail. To let him grasp her finger with his adorable gray paw. To draw a measure of comfort snuggling him against her cheek.

But it was not to be. After another step, Dexter changed his mind and darted into the bushes.

"Aw, too bad, buddy. I really could use a cuddle right about now." Staring after him for a moment, her gaze rose to the rock wall rising at the back of the pool where Simon had gone diving for the treasure chest. There didn't seem to be anything new or different about it at all. Same ferns clinging to life on ledges. Same water falling. She shrugged her shoulders as if someone could see her besides herself and God.

God created this beautiful oasis, hadn't He? Not some random act of the universe, like her parents had taught her to believe. A loving, kind, forgiving Father, Simon had called Him. She longed to taste a bit of that kind of faith.

He could tell Simon was being dishonest with him. About part or all of the story behind the photo, Gregory couldn't be sure. But seeing them side-by-side, Fern and Simon taking a stand together, finally working as a team, warmed his steely heart.

Had he made this next clue too hard for them to understand? The bread crumbs were there, if Fern used that amazing mind of hers and could connect them all.

He radioed Turner back at base camp. "I'm going to stay in the shadows for a while. Let me know if anything drastic happens up there."

"Ten-four, boss man."

Gregory sensed a touch of frustration in Turner's reply. He didn't blame him, really. Two more crew members had quit this morning. And having the medic/rescue team bored and breathing down his neck all day didn't help anything. He had to keep the momentum going, enough to hurtle Fern and Simon across the finish line.

Tonight's challenge would lead to tomorrow's. By then, they would have all the necessary letters to solve the final clue. A few more steps, and they'd all be there. At the finish line, crossing as a unified whole, emptier of their burdens, and a million dollars richer.

His cell phone jingled in his shirt pocket. He withdrew it and looked at the caller ID. Pops. Again. Eventually, he would have to face the firing squad for his disappearance. His father had undoubtedly found the note Gregory left detailing the television show, the strangely allocated funds, and Gregory's resignation.

He missed his mother more than anything else he'd left behind. Yes, she was spoiled and complacent. But she was his mother and not talking to her since his unexpected departure from the office bothered him.

He pressed the ignore button and set the tones to silent. Later. He'd deal with the family mess later. Only a few more days and he'd prove to everyone that his lifelong dream could be a successful reality. He shot his new agent, Brady, a quick text. **Gearing up for the final showdown. May finish earlier than expected. Any networks interested yet?**

For a good twenty seconds, he held his breath and waited for a return. Nothing came through, so he shoved the phone back in his pocket and headed for a perch up the hill from Simon and Fern's camp well accustomed to his footprints by now. Fern had almost caught him lurking in the shadows a couple times, but until nightfall he couldn't risk finding a new area. It would have to do.

He loved watching the interaction between Fern and Simon when they thought they were alone with the cameras. When he was in their presence, their rigid postures and tight muscles in the jaw lines betrayed their unease. But once he was "gone," they lounged near the fire and talked in quiet, easy voices. They couldn't see it yet. Didn't know what he knew about them. In casual moments, he suspected they sensed it coming, though. Like when Simon had looped his arm over her shoulders earlier. Soon the love train would smack them both in the forehead and they would be forever changed.

Simon rose to follow Fern. It was taking her far too long to come back. Ever since the copperhead run-in, he'd kept an even closer eye on her. And been more careful with his feet and his seat.

The meal the snake provided was such a boost to their confidence, though. And everyone on TV was right. Snake had tasted like chicken. He stopped short at the edge of their camp and sighed. Fern's dark head appeared first and then the rest of her trim form. She flashed him a smile and a small wave.

"Everything okay?"

"Uh, yeah. Just wondering where you were." A blush crept onto his cheeks. Had she noticed him staring?

"I don't see anything down there, but when he wanted us to hike out of camp before, we knew it by the way the riddle was worded. What do you think?"

It still warmed his insides when she asked his

opinion or needed his help. Thinking back to their first day, he'd never have guessed she would ever rely on him. "I think you're right. I've been thinking about it while you were gone. Remember the last line, don't dream?"

She nodded.

"Well, he gave us a flashlight on that last challenge. And now he mentioned a dream. What if the next clue is only available after dark?"

"That would make everything even harder." She chewed on her bottom lip. "Sounds like Gregory, so that's probably it. Anything he can do to take us to the edge of sanity and safety, right?"

He chuckled, grabbing onto the sweet tinkle of her laughter and hugging it close. When the challenge was over, and he was alone, he would pull these memories up and replay them on the film reel of his mind. "In that case, I guess there's nothing left to do but wait until nightfall."

"I'm pretty sure I saw Dexter. He looked fat and happy."

"That's great." He flashed a grin. "Have you checked on your birds yet today?"

Fern sputtered and lowered the drinking pot. Pink crept up her cheeks. "You knew about that?"

He winked. "They would have been little chicken nuggets. Yummy little chicken nuggets."

"I'm sorry, Simon. I couldn't kill them."

Part of what drew him to her was the fact that she was so caring. Prickly on the outside, soft and mushy on the inside. Like a beautiful cactus. "It's okay. I'm glad you didn't."

Fern dipped her head.

He took a step forward. She was a magnet, a strong force pulling at his internal compass. If he let his guard down, he could close the gap between them in a few short paces. Could wrap her in his arms and press his nose to her scalp. Could grasp her chin and turn her full lips toward his . . .

"You okay?" she asked again.

Not in the tiniest, least, little bit. He swallowed hard. "Yep." Turning on his good foot, he retraced his steps and plunked down beside the fire.

They spent the rest of the day lounging around the fire, re-hydrating, and napping. Every time he closed his eyelids, he pictured Fern. Down to the smallest details of the way her hips curved or her shoulders moved under her shirt.

There was a charge in the muggy air he couldn't quite identify. Maybe it was the end on its way. Maybe it was his almost-out-of-control emotions. He wished he could say it was all downhill from here, but he knew Gregory had more tricks up his sleeve. And there wasn't a doubt in his mind that the end of the challenge would be exponentially harder.

The sun drifted behind their mountains and the impenetrable black he had come to appreciate was soon upon them. Fern helped him to his feet. She shone the yellowish light ahead, and he attempted to follow without stumbling. At the pool he'd come to think of as Crystal Cove, they paused. The flashlight beam reflected off the top of the water like a mirror, too weak to penetrate to its depths, casting an eerie, playful glow about them.

"Do you see anything?"

He shook his head. "No. You?"

She swung the beam onto the face of the cliff and away again, into the dense scrub brush that made up the creek's banks. Out of the corner of his eye, he thought he noticed something. Once he turned his head fully toward the cliff face, though, it appeared to vanish. Again, he let his gaze soften and saw faint, greenish markings on the rocks. "Fern, tell me I'm not crazy."

"I see it too."

"Glow-in-the-dark paint?"

"I think so. But how do we get up there?"

Simon wrinkled his brow. How indeed. "What was the line about dangling?"

"Above the fall, dangle, don't dream."

He groaned. A nighttime hike that ended in a midnight rappelling adventure down the cliff face? Was Gregory insane? Or were they?

"Only one way to find out, I guess."

Once again, he followed her lead as she tiptoed along the curve of the base of the cliff until they were at the point where they'd entered all those weeks ago. There was no way he could make such a steep climb in the knee brace. His leg did feel much better, but was it ready to work without added support? "Only one way to find out," he mumbled.

"What?"

"Nothing." He undid the Velcro straps and tossed the brace to the side. He gently tested his full weight on the leg and, finding it stable, took a small step. Only minor pain, like a throbbing headache, radiated from the joint.

Fern frowned. "Are you sure?"

"I'll be careful. Take it nice and easy, and I should be fine."

They reached the summit faster than he anticipated, with his knee handling everything well. Boy, steroids were miracle drugs, weren't they? No way it would hold out in a wrestling match or a trampoline class, but he'd take it. "Do you see anything?"

"I'm not sure. I think there's something up ahead." She stopped and waited for him to catch up.

He placed a steadying hand on her shoulder and peered in the direction of the flashlight beam. "What is that?"

"I'm afraid to find out."

He squeezed around her and approached the strange jumble of items. Their purpose became clear when he knelt on his good leg to inspect them.

"Well?"

"It looks like he means to have one of us lower down to the clues on this." He held up a board, stout ropes strung through holes on either end like an old-fashioned bosun's chair. He traced the line to the sturdy tree where it was tied. Another line rose from the ground, through a massive brass pulley, and lay free on the ground. "That one's meant to be the belay line, I think." He pursed his lips. Fern had been doing much of the heavy lifting since he hurt his knee. It was his turn to put his neck on the line. He picked up the seat and fastened the seatbelt-like strap over his lap. "I'm ready."

"You should let me. What about your knee? You can't afford to injure it again."

"Won't need my knee. Just my seat and my eyes." He smiled. "I'll be fine."

She shoved the flashlight into his free hand. "Please be careful."

Her pale face and wide eyes made his stomach quake. He bit his cheek and nodded, squelching the urge to pull her to his chest.

At the edge of the cliff, he tested the line. "Cinch it up some, please." He could no longer see Fern, but the line went taut. "Here goes nothing."

Before he had a chance to contemplate the fact that he was thirty feet off the ground with a bum knee, his feet were dangling over the clear, summer air. *Lord, help Fern. I'm a lot heavier than her*. Not as heavy as when they started at least. He chuckled. The rope slipped through the pulley above him at a slow but steady pace, gently lowering him in front of the smooth cliff face. He held the flashlight in his mouth and gripped the ropes on either side of him with a ferocity that surprised him. He wasn't afraid of heights. Why the uncanny fear? He shook his head and concentrated on watching for the glowing clue to appear before him.

It felt almost like flying, he imagined. Hanging in the wind with nothing beneath him but a sturdy board. The water below him reflected the moonlight like a painting. One in which the artist was liberal with her soft strokes of rose, peach, and coral. Velvety. As if he could caress each patch of color like a smooth tile. It would be soft like Fern's hair gliding through his fingertips. Supple like her lips pressed against his. His stomach stirred, awakening to the thought of her lovely eyes and her need for someone to help her through the demons of her past. Someone to protect her, surround her with safety and love.

He almost missed the clue as it slowly passed by his nose, so lost in thoughts of Fern he had been. "Stop!" The bosun's chair jerked to a halt. He switched off the flashlight and looked at the strange symbol brushed on with glow-in-the-dark paint. It brought to mind an inverted triangle with uneven sides and had a set of three wavy lines in the middle. All of this was surrounded by a larger, uneven circle. To the left of the circle were five large dots in a line parallel to the wavy lines. What in the world did that mean? He pressed his eyes closed and committed the pattern to memory. "Okay! Lower me down!"

The chair didn't move. Had Fern not heard him? He yelled again and still there was no response. A slight breeze riffled the hair on the back of his neck.

His heart picked up its pace. "Fern!" Where was she? The line trembled. He could feel it in the fibers of the wood. And before he could scream again, he was plummeting toward the pool below. He slammed into water as hard as a two by four, sweeping his breath away as he struggled to loosen the strap around his waist. The moonlight played, dancing silver streaks in the water, surrounding him with the feeling of being trapped in a bubble. The only sounds that reached his ears were the pounding of the waterfall beating the pool into submission and the hammering of his heart.

He dug into the knot. It only tightened with each movement. Water filled his ear canals, pressing on his eardrums. Precious air escaped and tickled his nose before floating peacefully to the surface. He had to get free! He thrust his hand into his left pocket and curled his fingers around the knife Gregory had given them in the last challenge. A few minutes more and he would have to breathe whether his mind wanted to or not. His throat pulled, begging his mouth to open. He sawed frantically at the rope binding him to the board, to the weight of the heavy cords pinning him to the bottom. He had to get to Fern. What if the bear had come back? He didn't remember much about that encounter, but he definitely remembered it being angry.

At last, his restraints broke. He rocketed to the surface and gasped, stars dancing at the periphery of his vision. His knee throbbed as he tried to propel himself to land. He flopped onto the bank, sucking in the precious, clean air and cradling his knee in his quivering hands. That was the second time this life-giving pool had tried to kill him.

Chapter 18

The moon climbed high enough to break free of the eastern mountains. A slow, black marble being filled with molten gold crawling through the sky. Her hand burned from lowering Simon over the cliff edge, but he wasn't as heavy as she'd worried he might be. The pulleys relieved much of the pressure. A breeze rustled the leaves and cooled her flushed cheeks. Leaning against the tree, she closed her eyes and waited for Simon's signal to continue.

A twig popped nearby.

Her eyes flew open. The moon's light appeared so bright it hardly felt like nighttime. She peered into the bushes several feet away. Something moved. The silvery glint of light reflected from something metallic. Goosebumps sped up her arms. Someone was watching her. Again. If it was Gregory, she was about fed up with it. Weren't his zillion cameras enough for him? What kind of sick pleasure did he get from seeing their suffering firsthand? It was time to end this charade. She balled her fists. "I know you're there." The black lump in the bushes grew a little larger but didn't move into plain view. What if it wasn't Gregory? What if some backwoods hermit with an extreme aversion to strangers and an affinity for hiding bodies had been watching them?

She looped the excess rope around the tree and tied it onto itself. She took a step toward the bush, and the person hiding there jumped up, spun away from her, and fled into the forest. He wasn't going to get away so easily. She was sick of this ridiculous cat and mouse, predator-prey feeling. Leaping over a downed tree, she gave chase. The person's broad shoulders and narrow waist clued her in to the fact it was indeed a man, but he was too far away to be sure whether it was Gregory or not. Under ordinary circumstances, Fern still wouldn't have been able to catch the phantom fleeing twenty feet in front of her. He gained ground, seemingly flying through the forest. Fern doubled over and planted her hands on her knees. Stars danced on the ground, black closing in, suffocating her. Running was a bad idea. Dehydrated, nearly-starved heart and lungs didn't much like exercise. Her watery legs trembled. She sank to the ground, gasping for air.

If it was Gregory, why on earth was he out here? What could he possibly gain? She remembered the whispers of the camera crew at the waterfall. Each of their voices holding a tinge of fear. And the uneasiness of the paramedic and rescue crew. A shiver of fear shimmied up her spine. She didn't know much about psychopaths. Should she and Simon be more concerned by Gregory's odd personality? About the extreme nature of his challenges? About the fact that he seemed unwilling to let them go home, even in the face of injury?

She eased onto her back, laced her fingers behind her head, and stared at the glimpse of sky peeking through the canopy. Every one of her cells was depleted. She had to get up. Had to get back to Simon. But even the effort of bending her legs to rise seemed too much. Had her body already started utilizing muscle for nutrition? Probably. The few meals they'd had certainly weren't enough. Earthworm stew, a few minnows, a couple crawdads, a half a sandwich, a snake, beef jerky, peanut butter, and tuna. Hardly enough for a days' worth of protein, let alone half a month.

"Fern!" Simon's panicked voice filtered through the trees.

How? Shouldn't he still be dangling from the cliff? Her stomach muscles trembled as she rose to a seated position. "Over here!"

His heavy steps clunked closer. "Fern?"

She raised her hand to flag him down. "Right here."

He rushed to her and dropped to his knees. "What happened? Are you okay?"

Why wouldn't she be? She wrinkled her brow.

"Why are you wet?"

His lips quirked into a lopsided frown. "Why are you fifty feet from the rope you were supposed to be holding onto?"

"Someone was out here. Watching me from the shadows."

"And you decided to investigate?"

Why did he sound so angry? "Yes. I'm sick of being spied on. We signed up for a television show, not a stalker."

He jumped to his feet so quickly, Fern recoiled. "We are a team. And you left me dangling on a board twenty feet off the ground."

"I . . . I'm sorry. I tied the rope off. I was coming right back." Didn't he understand? She had to find out who was out there watching them.

"I nearly drowned. Again. Wouldn't that be a nice surprise when you finished gallivanting around the forest?"

His sarcasm pierced through her armor. She bristled. "Wouldn't it be a nice surprise for you to find me murdered by some backwoods creep?"

"You're impossible! You're never wrong, are you? Dr. Strongbow, ice queen, master of the forest. Strong, independent, lonely Fern."

Tears pricked her eyes.

"Do you wonder why you are all alone, Fern?"

She clenched her teeth so tight she thought they might crack.

"Do you ever wonder why no one can stand to be

in your life? You think you are stronger alone. That you can protect yourself easier alone, don't you?"

She didn't dare move. She wouldn't justify him with an answer.

"Don't you understand when you push everyone away, you're hurting yourself more than helping? You've done nothing but put up walls since we've been out here. I've tried, Fern. I really have."

Once he picked up steam to his current pace, it seemed he couldn't halt the train of words. He had been biting his tongue for weeks, hadn't he? Her heart ached. She wanted to beg him to stop. To quit spouting truths that felt like icicles stabbing her. But she couldn't speak over her dry tongue and breaking heart.

"I've been as patient as I can. This is the last straw, though. If you care more about your own self-interests than my safety, I can't be your partner any more. I can't finish this and just hope you've got my back. You're watching out for your own back. I wanted that to be my job. Don't you get it?"

He grabbed both her biceps and pulled her to her feet. She deserved the pinches of pain his grip sent shooting down her arms. The moonlight reflected the emotion in his dilated, vulnerable eyes.

"Don't you get that I love you? And it's hopeless, because you will never be able to believe that a man, any man, this man could possibly love you." His voice dropped to a whisper. "Can you?"

He was pleading, begging her to understand. But he was the one who didn't get it. She dropped her gaze.

He didn't know her well enough to love her. She was too broken. He deserved the truth. If she told him, then he would be free to hate her. He'd have all the facts, and there was no way he'd still feel whatever he was feeling.

"Simon," her voice hitched. "You don't understand—"

"I knew it." He dropped his arms and spun away from her.

The disgust in his voice released the flood of tears. She deserved every word. He was right. "You can't love me, Simon." She touched his shoulder with a fingertip.

He pulled back. "That's exactly it, Dr. Strongbow. It's not your decision to make." He stomped away.

Each step he took nailed another wound into her chest. She sank to her knees and cradled her face in her hands. Her sobs echoed through the silent, dark forest. A cloud floated in front of the moon. Perfect. Not even the silvery orb of light could stand to look at her.

He'd gone too far. He shouldn't have lost control and let those awful words loose. His throat constricted. "I'm so sorry, Fern." Only the tree he leaned against heard his whispered concession.

Someone had been watching them? Gregory? But why?

His shoulders slumped. It didn't matter. And no matter how mad he was, he couldn't leave Fern out here alone all night. He snorted. She'd probably prefer it, but he wouldn't give her the satisfaction of making him worry all night long.

He snuck back to her but stopped short when her muffled cries reached his ears. His heart fluttered. He'd caused those tears. He swallowed hard. He hadn't meant to say he loved her. Where had the thoughts even come from? But as he watched her huddled on the ground, he knew they were true.

Love is patient. Love is kind.

He had been neither. What a jerk he was! *Lord, forgive me.*

The cloud cover swept away, restoring the moon's dawn-like glow. He stole closer with tiny steps. Touched her shoulder. And waited. She didn't seem surprised by his presence, but when she turned her teary eyes toward him, his heart nearly jerked from his chest. What could he say that would make any of his hurtful words better? He pulled Fern gently to her feet and wrapped his arms around her. She trembled, but her sobs ceased. He kissed the top of her head and sighed. "Forgive me, Fern. I'm so sorry."

She pulled back and retreated several paces. "There's something you need to know about me."

"I'm a murderer. Not like you. A real one." She

absentmindedly brought her hand to her stomach. He took in a slow breath, and she waited for his judgment for what seemed like forever. Precisely why she'd never had the courage to confess to anyone before her monumental sins.

"How far along were you?"

"Six weeks." The weight of things she'd needed to get off her chest for more than a decade threatened to suffocate her. The floodgates of the past opened. "You know the worst part?" She chuckled mirthlessly. "There were a lot of worst parts. But the really awful part? It wasn't the physical pain—and trust me it hurt like nothing I've ever felt before or since." She looked at her fidgeting hands. "They made me see the baby's heartbeat. I wish I'd had the courage to stop everything then, you know? Having the baby would have changed everything. And I was so scared. But not having him changed everything too. It was one of those times in your life when no matter which road you take, you can't ever be the same again." A tear trickled down her nose. "Except the road I chose, I suffered alone. No one knew what I went through. Why I couldn't sleep. The guilt that haunted my every breath."

Simon took her hand and squeezed.

"Everyone is always talking about abortion. The big issue. The politics. The morality of it all. No one stops to consider how someone like me might feel. I've been terrified someone would find out and hate me. That my deepest, darkest secret would be flung into the world and I'd be alone again. After everyone found out what a monster I was, no one would ever be able to love me again. Never be able to forgive me for what I'd done." She shrugged. "I wouldn't blame them. I've never forgiven myself. I think about it now and I wonder why I couldn't keep him. It wouldn't have been so bad to have a little baby to love."

"What about Scott? What did he say?"

She snorted. "It was his idea. I went to him and told him. He never blinked. Just handed me cash and said, 'Take care of it.' At first, I didn't know what to do, but he called me every day for a week. Told me everyone would hate me. That they'd laugh. Maybe even my parents would disown me. I'd never graduate and go to vet school. It was like he had this way about him that everything he said was rule. And I let myself believe him because I wanted so badly for someone to tell me what to do. To make everything disappear. I wanted him to still love me. But he didn't. He never loved me in the first place. I was a fool. An alone, terrified, stupid fool."

"Fern, look at me."

She wiped her sticky face and looked from the tops of her eyes.

He placed his index finger on her chin and tipped her face up. "You are not a monster. Scott was wrong. You made a mistake, yes. And not everyone would understand. But God still wants a relationship with you."

"I'm not worthy."

"No one is."

"I don't deserve forgiveness." She didn't deserve God or Simon. She should be miserable for the rest of her life for what she'd done.

"Yes, you do."

She shook her head. "I don't have enough faith."

"Yes, you do." He smiled for the first time all night. "I will pray that you find it."

"Diary cam entry number I-have-no-idea." Fern wiped the sweat from her upper lip with her index finger. "Being out here has changed me. The last couple days have been different. I don't know if you can see it or not. It's like I've released some of the things I've kept in to fly free with the trees and the breeze." She chuckled. "That was almost as bad as one of Gregory's clues. Sorry about that, people of America.

"I couldn't have asked for a better partner. Simon has been supportive and kind, even when I couldn't treat myself the same way. And when I let him down.

"We both feel a change coming on the wind. Maybe it's because we are approaching day thirty. Maybe it's because we are starving and a bit delusional. Either way, we must be getting close to the end."

She closed the camera, ending the recording, and smiled. Simon didn't act like he hated her after the truth. And it was such a relief to get it off her chest.

Like a tiny portion of the burden was given to him, and she didn't have to suffer under its full weight any more.

Simon dreamed of the strange sign on the cliff face. His first thought when he peeled his eyes open was of its meaning. His stomach rumbled, and his mouth watered as he caught a phantom whiff of coffee and cinnamon rolls.

He was ready to go home. All but his heart. It wanted to be where ever Fern was.

Fern's confession the night prior had driven any remaining anger toward her far away. No wonder she was always trying to protect herself. Not only had she been conned into giving her innocence to a man who pretended to care for her, she'd been coerced to . . . He couldn't finish the thought. How much worse had it been for her living with such a painful secret? He wanted to tell her it was okay. That she had been a kid and made a stupid mistake, but something held his tongue. She needed the comfort to come from the Father he knew would forgive her. *Lord, help Fern find You. Above all else, help her find Your loving embrace.* He couldn't imagine the mental angst she had hidden from everyone half her life.

"Morning," Fern greeted him as she returned to camp.

"Morning." He wanted to grab her down-turned

face and make her look at him. Make her see he held no judgment against her. Make her see herself the way he saw her. The intense emotions he felt for her had rather snuck up on him. But now that he had acknowledged them, he realized he didn't want to live again without them. *To have loved and lost is better than never having loved at all.* He grinned. Whoever coined that phrase knew what he was talking about.

He yawned, stretched, and smiled at her. "I'm hungry."

She giggled. "You're always hungry."

Wasn't that the truth? At least he'd made her smile. There wasn't a day out here he could say he wasn't hungry sometime during the long hours. Sometimes he couldn't even remember why they were out there in the first place. There were moments, like this one, he felt almost normal again. Then the past would come snaking in and drag him into its dark, suffocating belly. When he left this challenge, he'd still be the same man. Would anyone really see him differently?

A squirrel barked in the branches overhead. The first one he'd seen or heard in days.

Their presence had done exactly what he'd feared, driven away most of the wildlife. His ears perked as he attempted to track the gray blur's stealthy movements overhead. He reached for the bow and arrows near his seat and notched one into the string.

The squirrel paused, raised his sun umbrella, and gnawed on an acorn.

Simon let out a slow breath and fired. The squirrel didn't suffer, dead before it fell from the branch.

"Wow! What a shot!" Fern retrieved the animal.

Maybe it wouldn't matter so much how the world saw him after the show. His chest swelled as he took the limp creature from her hand. "Breakfast is served, madam."

She smiled, and for the briefest of moments, her gaze flicked to meet his eyes. He hoped she saw what he felt written there. If Fern could find a way to love herself, maybe there was a chance for him too.

They worked in tandem to prepare breakfast. His mouth watered again as the savory aroma of the meat mixed with wild mushrooms and plantain wafted from the pot. He sketched the symbol into the ground while they waited. "Do you have any thoughts?"

She shook her head. How could someone who hadn't had access to shampoo, soap, or clean clothes in nearly a month still be so beautiful?

Had he made this clue too hard? Gregory scooted closer to the screens he now monitored alone. Other than Turner and the paramedic/rescue crew on standby, everyone else had quit. Good riddance.

Nothing stirred in Fern and Simon's camp.

He was going to have to send in another clue. They were running out of time.

Rubbing his elbow, sore from falling in the forest while Fern chased him, he leaned back in the chair. What could he do to help without being obvious?

His cell phone vibrated in his pocket, and he nearly tipped the leaning chair to the floor. Without glancing at the caller ID, he pressed talk. "Hello."

Pops let out a string of expletives that would have made a sailor blush. "It is about time you saw fit to humble yourself and answer that blasted phone. Where on this green earth are you? Your mother is worried sick."

He'd been so careful to screen his calls. What a rookie mistake he'd made this lovely morning. "Hi, Pops. I—"

"You can't up and quit and never come back, son. I make the rules around here. You've got some serious explaining to do."

Two weeks of freedom from his father's reptilian grasp had done Gregory good. He couldn't remember the last day he'd tied a noose around his neck or put loafers on his feet. Gregory wiggled his toes, rather enjoying the feeling of the air through his new sandals. "You know what, Pops? I don't care."

If silence could scream, Gregory would be deaf.

"I've been your good little heir for too long. Never questioned your rein. Your tactics. Followed the plan you laid out for my future to a tee. I'm done."

"Gregory Zachary Vanderbilt the—"

"I don't want to hear it. Nothing you can say will change my mind. Thank you for all you've done for me, but until you are ready to accept I'm a grown man capable of planning my own future, I don't want another red cent from you. I'll pay back every penny I owe for the television station."

"You can't be serious, son."

"As a heart attack, as they say. I'm done, Pops. It's as simple as that. I never wanted your life. I'm happy for the first time I can ever remember. Give Mom a kiss for me. I'll be happy to see her when I'm done filming."

"Son—"

"When you accept me for me, I'll be happy to see you too." Gregory ended the call and took a deep breath. His hands shook and his heart pounded, but a smile spread on his face so big his cheeks hurt. That. Felt. Good.

Chapter 19

It had been four mornings since she'd told Simon her truth. And he still hadn't said a word about it. She couldn't blame him. There really wasn't much to be said. She disgusted him and the feelings he thought he had were dead. End of story. That was that.

She crawled out of the shelter and tossed one of its fallen sticks aside. Simon's shelter was empty again for the third morning in a row. His bow and arrow also gone. Though he'd been hunting every morning, the squirrel had been the only successful kill. Her stomach was again rumbling and voicing its concern over her lack of caloric intake. Did they really have ten whole days left?

Every morning she stared at the sign sketched into the ground. And she was sick of it. Sick of trying to figure it out. Sick of even thinking about it at all. Couldn't Gregory give them a break and help a little bit? Without much else to do, she grabbed the blackened pot and made her way to the creek. As she bent down to scoop some fresh water, the dizziness she was almost getting used to set in. She plopped on a large, round rock and hung her head, waiting for the episode to pass. She wanted to sprawl in the sunshine and close her eyes. Instead, she filled the pot and hefted it to her waist. Same amount of water, somehow heavier today. She strolled toward the waterfall, keeping her eyes peeled for edible plants. They'd pretty much exhausted all the greens near camp.

She stopped to rest and listen to the soothing splash of water sliding over the cliff. The symbol no doubt still glowed above her, but it was completely invisible in the daylight. She grabbed a stick and doodled in the softer earth near the water. Repeating the sign over and over, large, small, medium, rotated on its axis a hundred different ways. It would never make sense. She looked at the nearest camera and pasted on a sickly-sweet smile. "Gregory, dear, I know you're watching. This stupid symbol doesn't make any sense." The last words ground out through her clenched teeth. It took all her reserve not to scream. With her left foot, she kicked the dirt, marring the symbols, erasing her drawings.

Wait. She stopped before she cleared the last sketch. She had drawn it oriented the way Simon said it was on the wall. The lopsided triangle looked a bit like an arrow. What if the wavy lines represented the waterfall and the tip of the triangle was the direction they should travel? And the circle was supposed to represent a hole or a cave or something. But how far did Gregory want them to hike? And how would they know when they'd arrived?

Simon's muffled call came from the direction of camp.

"Down here!"

A few minutes later he stepped to her side, a frown etched on his face.

"No luck?"

He shook his head.

She smiled, genuinely this time. "I think I may have an idea. Look at this." She explained her theory. "The only problem is I don't know how far we will have to go to find whatever is next."

"I think you are onto something. Good job."

His praise warmed her. Fizzy champagne buoyed her self-esteem. "Well, come on then. No time like the present."

"Nothing else to do, so why not?"

They leap-frogged across the stream atop partially submerged rocks. For the first time in days, Fern felt a bit lighter. Maybe telling Simon her secret wasn't the end of the world? Simon plowed to a stop, and she crashed into his back. She placed both hands on his shoulder blades. His muscles tensed under her touch, hardened and toned from the exertion they'd expended out here. Her breath fluttered.

"Five dots, right?"

"Yes." What was he getting at?

He thrust out his right arm and pointed. "A."

"What?" Did he need a drink of water? Because he wasn't making any sense whatsoever.

He gently nudged her around to stand in front of him and pointed again at a straight-trunked tulip poplar. "See the A carved in the trunk? It has five dots next to it."

"Yes! The five dots represent how far we go?"

"Exactly. And we get more letters. What do you think it spells?"

Death. She shoved the thought aside. They'd already covered the topic of Gregory being out to kill them and dismissed it as foolishness. Hadn't they? Besides, if they still had four more trees to find, four more letters would be far too much for that one creepy word. "I don't know."

"Okay, so," Simon glanced over his shoulder and moved his lips as he silently counted, "we're about, what, fifty feet from the creek?"

She nodded.

"Assuming they are evenly spaced, we shouldn't have to go very far to find the rest. Right?"

"Right." She hoped. Her sponge-legs weren't up for a long hike today. Unless it led her to a steak and baked potato.

She let Simon lead the way, with his half-hitched gait favoring the bum knee. He hadn't said anything about his fall, but she knew it had aggravated things again. She felt awful that she had hurt him. Her headstrong days were behind her. Hopefully.

She scanned the nearby trees. Without any sort of directional marking to tell them which fifty feet away to head, they could be searching for hours. Or not. "There!" She pointed to another tulip poplar a dozen or so feet to the left. "O."

"Good eye." He winked and nudged her with his elbow. "C'mon."

Sparklers flared in her tummy. She avoided his gaze and looked instead to the trunks. In short order they found two more letters, M and E, each evenly spaced. "That leaves one."

"Good thing, too, 'cause I'm awful thirsty."

Their summer stay had not given them an inch of leeway on temperature. Nearly every day had been sweltering and muggy. Did she even remember what air conditioning felt like? She wiped her brow with the hem of her filthy shirt and swallowed what little spit remained in her sandpaper mouth.

"I think I see something."

He pointed at an ancient pine tree, its tip appearing to pierce the sky. Apparently the circle wasn't a cave but the round trunk of a tree. Was it an oversight that the first four clues were on poplar trees and this one a pine? She doubted it. Gregory was far too clever and far too consistent to mess up. The bright orange S was neatly tucked under an arrow pointing directly up the trunk. The lowest whorl of branches sprouted at eye level. "I'll climb."

Simon opened his mouth and clamped it shut again. He nodded tersely.

"I can tell by the limp your knee is bugging you. And it's partly my fault. I don't mind. I'm a regular ole monkey. Watch me."

Her joke earned a half-hearted chuckle.

"Give me a boost?"

Simon placed his hands around her waist and lifted her like an ice skater lifts his partner. Easily, fluidly. She grabbed the lowest branch and chinned-up until she could throw her foot over it. Straddling the branch, she smiled at him. "Be back in a jiffy." The branches might have well been designed by a ladder engineer so easy were they to mount. The ground and Simon both soon disappeared behind a curtain of fragrant needles. The sticky trunk went on forever. Maybe this was Jack's beanstalk in disguise. Gradually the tree's girth lessened, and Fern found the branches thinner. How much farther could it possibly be? She stopped to rest on a flexing branch and wiped the sweat from her eyes. As she craned her neck to view the top of the tree, a breeze rattled the limbs and sunlight reflected off something tied to a ribbon a few feet above.

Her energy renewed, she made the last hurdles effortlessly and untied the ribbon. A brass skeleton key with an E carved into the handle. What could it possibly open out here? Her heart bounced into her throat. Could this be the final clue? Skeleton keys opened chests. Right? "I found something!"

"Good! Be careful coming down!"

She looped the ribbon around her neck and began

her descent. Easy enough. Somehow, though, she ended up on the far side of the tree. Obviously this side had taken the brunt of the years of storms and wind. Many of the branches were broken and all that remained of some were jagged knobs. She needed to work her way back to the easy side. The ground, filled with yellow and brown pine needles, peeked through the remaining branches between her and land. She stretched a bit too far to plant her right leg on the next lower branch and teetered. In her rush to right herself, she brought the left foot down hard. Her grip loosened as the branch holding all her weight cracked and snapped off. She fell like a sack of stones, arms flailing for something, anything to hold onto.

One of the broken branches snagged her shirt sleeve, slowing her fall for a brief moment. It tore into the vulnerable flesh under her arm. Fern yelped in pain moments before she slammed into the ground. The breath flew from her lungs. Simon appeared before her with wide eyes. She stuttered over ragged breaths that didn't fill her sucker-punched lungs. "My arm. Is it bad?" She tried to lift it to see for herself, but it wouldn't cooperate with her commands.

Simon glanced at it. His face blanched.

"Help me see."

He lifted her arm and gently turned her head. Blood poured from the wound, yet she had no pain. She knew in a heartbeat, as the blood ebbed and spouted with her pulse, she had lacerated the brachial artery. It was either risk losing her arm or die.

"Tourniquet. Now." She couldn't manage many more instructions with her pasty mouth. With the good arm, she pointed to Simon's belt.

He yanked it off and looped it around her bicep, under the level of the shoulder.

"Tighter."

Fern clenched her teeth as he cinched it to the smallest notch. "Tighter."

Looping it a second time, his hands shook as he pulled it even snugger.

"That'll do." She bit back the bile rising in her throat. "I'm going to die, Simon."

His brows pinched. "Don't say that. Don't you dare even think it."

"It's bad, Simon. If Gregory isn't already on his way, it's too late."

"He is. I'm sure he is. Your camera is still on. He knows." Tears pooled in the corners of his eyes.

She used the last bit of strength she had to smile and whisper, "Pray with me?"

Before Simon finished his heartfelt plea, Fern's eyes slid closed behind deathly pale lids. "Lord, please!" He turned his face to the sky, letting the sun grace the tears sliding down his cheeks. What could he do? Even if he carried Fern to base camp, by the time he made it she'd be gone. "We need a miracle, Lord."

A definite rumble reached his ears. His pulse

quickened. The dark blur of a helicopter zipped past the treetops. Due east. With his heart thrumming loudly in his ears, he scooped Fern's limp form into his arms and raced toward it. Though he couldn't remember exactly what it looked like, with the bright, pompous colors on its side, the helicopter had to belong to Gregory. It simply had to. He gritted his teeth and stepped over a log. His knee throbbed, but he didn't care. Gregory had to have landed nearby. If Simon could only get Fern there, they could have her at the hospital in minutes. His ACL or patella or other minor tendons he didn't know the names of could tear clean in two for all he cared.

"Come on, Fern. Stay with me." Was she still breathing? He nudged her cheek, nestled against his shoulder. A faint wisp of air brushed his earlobe. Barely. He had to hurry. Had Gregory found somewhere to land?

"Hello!" Two distinct voices filtered through the trees ahead.

His heart leaped into his throat. He swallowed hard. "Over here!" Stumbling over logs and rocks in his hurry to reach the medics, his grip on Fern's fragile body never wavered. The same medic team and search and rescue lady, Amy, that attended to him waited a few feet ahead. The sounds of the forest faded away. He gently placed Fern onto their yellow stretcher and pulled his blood-stained, dirty arms away. Time froze as he stared at her unmoving features. "It's okay. You're going to be okay." He leaned close and whispered, "You can't die. You hear me? I love you."

The medics crowded around her, pushing him to the side. With his gaze glued to her face, he slumped backward, landing hard. The impact brought everything back into focus. The two-person team hovering above Fern calmly voiced directives to Amy, who held a large backpack open and offered the items requested. They placed an IV in Fern's good arm and started giving her fluids. Secured her to the stretcher with a series of heavy-duty Velcro straps.

"She's going to lose that arm," one of them said under his breath.

The second medic pressed his lips together and nodded.

No. This wasn't happening. Anger cleared the tears from his vision. Noticing Gregory for the first time standing to the side, Simon's fury flared. He pointed at their sheepish-looking director. "You." Simon closed the gap between them in three strides, and planted his hands on Gregory's polo shirt. "This is your fault!" He ground the words between rapid breaths. Before he knew what he was doing, Simon shoved Gregory backward into a massive oak. "You and your stupid game. Your ridiculous tasks."

Gregory's face paled, his lips bluing under the intense pressure of Simon's hands crushing his chest. Simon's nostrils flared. Gregory deserved it for what he'd done to Fern. He deserved to suffer like they had for three and a half weeks.

Gregory didn't fight back as his eyes bulged.

"Simon! Simon!"

Amy's screams finally pierced through the veil of red clogging Simon's thoughts. He blinked. What was he doing? Making the murderer title come true? He dropped his hands, stumbled backward, and collapsed, cradling his head between his hands.

Gregory gasped and coughed.

Amy laid a gentle hand on his shoulder. "Simon, look at me."

He slowly raised his head.

"We have to go. Now."

The medic team, with Fern between them, waited with mouths gaping.

He bolted to his feet. "I'm coming with you."

"There isn't room for you." Amy pointed to her chest, and then to the medics. "Let us do our job. She's in good hands."

He had to go with her. To make sure she was okay.

"I'll stay with you," Gregory offered.

Simon shot daggers at the trembling man.

Amy moved to Gregory and grabbed him by the elbow. "I don't think that's such a good idea. We are wasting too much time." She pulled Gregory alongside her, following the team carrying Fern. They melted into the trees.

Simon was alone.

In a matter of minutes, the helicopter passed overhead in the opposite direction, stirring the treetops to a frenzy. What was he supposed to do now? Go back to camp and sit on his hands and wait until someone came with an update? The thought turned his stomach.

Chapter 20

Gregory paced the same line on the tiled floor of the waiting room he'd been pacing for over two hours. How he hadn't worn a groove he couldn't be sure. He glanced at the time on his cell phone for at least the thousandth time. What was taking the surgeon so long? He gingerly rubbed the ribs on his left side. What would Simon do to him if they lost Fern? Hopefully they wouldn't have to find out.

The cell phone vibrated as he slipped it back into his pocket. "What?"

"Easy, tiger."

"Turner, did you talk to Simon?"

"I did."

"And?"

"I told him not to shoot the messenger but to stay put for now. He wasn't happy. But I did like you said and reminded him if he left, he'd be letting Fern down."

Gregory knew that would get to Simon. "Good, good."

"Any news there?"

"No—" A blue-scrubbed doctor with those funny blue slippers over his shoes stepped into the waiting area and locked gazes with him. "Hang on a sec." Gregory lowered the phone. "I'm with Dr. Strongbow."

The physician wiped his palm down his face.

Gregory's stomach plummeted. "Spit it out. Bad news?"

"Quite the opposite." The doctor's broad smile spanned the entire waiting room. "Do you believe in miracles, sir?"

"Excuse me?"

"Miracles. You know the kind from the man upstairs?" The doctor waggled a finger toward the ceiling.

Gregory frowned. "Not particularly."

"Well, it might be time to start."

"Oh, good grief. What are you getting at?"

"Dr. Strongbow's surgery went incredibly well. We do not believe she will lose the arm, nor do we believe she will suffer any long-term issues. I honestly can't explain it.

"We've given her blood, and I was able to repair the artery and external wounds. Of course, we can't be certain until she wakes and is able to communicate to us how well her arm works."

Gregory slumped into the nearest chair and sighed. Miracle indeed.

Fern tried to open her eyes and quickly recognized the effects of anesthesia playing in her swimming brain. Heavy eyelids closed over her eyes that couldn't seem to be still. She tried to lift her arm but found it impossible. The last thing she remembered was closing her eyes to the soothing sound of Simon's prayer and knowing she wasn't going to wake up. How was she still alive? And in a comfy bed no less?

Open, eyes. She gathered her eyebrows together and forced her lids to pry apart. Sterile lighting pierced her pupils, making her want to close them again. She moved the other arm, brought it at a snail's pace to shield her face, and squinted against the too-bright fluorescent bulbs. Surely someone in the hospital would have thought about the blaring light on eyes that had almost died. Couldn't someone dim them? She rotated her wrist and stared for a long minute at the green-winged IV needle pumping fluids into the back of her clean hand. The dirt resumed its dark coloring at her wrist, just beyond the reach of the clear tape.

What had happened? Oh, right. She had fallen and that spear of a tree limb had sliced her open. *God, why am I still here? Why didn't You let me die?*

The curtain at the end of her bed flew open, the metal loops attaching it to the frame swooshing as a red-haired lady with a big smile appeared. "Well, now, you're up. My name's Leesa. I've been watching over you post-surgery. You gave everyone quite a scare, ya know. The whole floor is buzzing about you."

"Why?" The simple word stung her parched throat.

"It's not every day someone brings a patient in a private helicopter. And especially not one with an injury quite like yours. We all had wages against you keeping that arm." Leesa's smile broadened. "I knew soon's I laid eyes on you, though, the good Lord would save you, and your arm too."

She'd been right about the brachial artery. How had they managed to save it?

Leesa busied herself checking the IV line and Fern's pulse, but her jabbering never paused. "I don't think we've ever seen anything quite like it. With that tourniquet, it should have been a no-brainer the arm would be too injured to save. You're a very blessed young lady. I can't wait to tell the others you're awake." Leesa skipped out of the bay, forgetting to close the curtain.

Fern blinked twice. *Lord, I didn't deserve this blessing. Why me?*

Quiet voices grew closer. A girl, with her hand on her bulging stomach, waddled into view. Fern met her gaze. The young lady smiled, grimaced, and grabbed her stomach. An older woman—her mother maybe—rubbed the girl's back and whispered platitudes. When the contraction passed, the girl resumed her slow walk past Fern's curtains and out of view.

Fern smiled even as tears sprang to her eyes. The girl looked to be about sixteen or seventeen. A sharp twinge tore through her. Why couldn't she have been braver back then? Would it have really been so bad to have her baby? He would have been so beautiful. So sweet. Tears poured down her cheeks, trickling under her gown. Silent sobs constricted her throat. River would have been eleven this year if she hadn't . . . She deserved to die. Why hadn't He taken her out at the tree? She could never make up for what she'd done. She didn't deserve any miracles. Any breaks in life. Any good thing at all. Her chest ached with the feeling of her heart shattering like a hot lightbulb touched by cold water. Shards of ugly glass stabbing into everything. There was no way to put the pieces back in place. No way to cauterize the bleeding internal wounds. *Lord, I wish I had died. Why, why, why did you leave me here? It hurts too much. Every time I think about what I did, the wound rips open fresh, gushing. What can I do?*

Fern's gaze was drawn to the decorations on the far wall. A simple wooden cross hung, with the words, Faith, Hope, and Love engraved on its arms, as if waiting for her to notice it. What did she know about those words? About the scripture reference beneath them? No one had taken the time to teach her about the Bible, but Simon's words came back to her.

Faith.

A well of invisible longing swirled in what was left of her broken heart. Churning until she could resist its urge no longer. Was it possible to be whole again? She dropped her chin to her chest and pressed her eyes closed. Slowed her breathing to a more regular rhythm, swallowing the hiccupping cries. *Lord, I'm so sorry. Please forgive me for the biggest mistake and regret of my life. I don't deserve Your love, but Simon said I could call on You. I'm so, so, so sorry. I don't really want to die. I want to love myself again. To be able to find that faith Simon talked about.*

A still, small voice stirred in her heart, urging her to release all her pain, fears, sadness, guilt, and regret to Him. Everything she'd kept hidden for more than a decade poured out with the fresh release of hot tears. The weight of the burden she'd carried lifted. She could almost picture it as a tangible black item, floating into God's outstretched hands. She'd done a terrible thing, but somehow, He still loved her. For the first time, she let His forgiveness wrap around her, fill her with a warmth unlike anything she'd ever known.

She would probably never be able to completely fill the void where her child should have been. Maybe she'd never be able to completely forgive herself, but it was suddenly so clear that God was more perfect than she'd ever hope to be. Where she couldn't forgive her atrocious past, His perfect love could. Her faith in His love could get her through the muddied, scarred past into the light of healing. *Thank you, Lord, for loving me when I can't even forgive myself. Help me move on.*

I'd really like to. I know you are taking good care of him up there, and when I die someday I'd like to meet my baby River.

Fern sighed, feeling more relief than she could remember ever feeling. Like her lungs hadn't expanded to their full capacity ever in her entire life. Her exhausted eyes slid closed, allowing the remaining effects of painkillers and stress to pull her into the first restful slumber in more than a decade.

When she woke, it was to the sound of someone clearing her throat. Fern's eyes opened more easily this time. It took a moment to focus on the brunette at her bedside. And a moment longer for recognition to dawn. "Amy, right?"

A smile lit up the woman's face. "Amy Evans." She held out her hand. "Oh, right. Sorry. Anyway, I was passing by and thought I'd stop in and check on you. I'm glad to see you're doing so well."

Fern returned the smile and pointed at the limp arm wrapped in a myriad of layered bandages. "I'm getting feeling back. Hurts like a beast." She chuckled.

"We thought we'd lost you, you know."

"That's what everyone keeps telling me." She still wasn't quite sure why God had spared her, but she was slowly coming to grips with the new feelings.

"I've been praying." Amy glanced at her shoes. "I don't think the way Mr. Vanderbilt is running things is quite right. There should have been more safety precautions."

"We knew what we were signing up for."

"I suppose that's true."

An awkward silence hung between them and filled the hollow space between ceiling and floor tiles. Sometime during her drugged nap, she'd been moved to a private room.

"I wanted to ask you something."

Fern raised her eyebrows.

"I've been in search and rescue for a little over a year now. I had my own survival experience, and for reasons I don't want to explain right now, but I am curious why you're putting yourself through this. Is the money really worth it?"

How many times had she asked herself that very same question in the last few hours? Then there was Simon. A grin crept onto her face and a tingle tickled her abdomen. They had lost the competition because of her accident, but what she'd gained was Simon. Money or not, knowing him was worth it. "Yes. I mean, no. Not the money. But it's all been worth it. Have they brought Simon in yet?"

"I'm sorry. I don't know. I can check if you like, but I have to run. It was nice meeting you, Fern Strongbow."

"Same to you. And thank you for helping me."

Amy slipped through the door, leaving Fern alone with her thoughts. Where was Simon? Why hadn't he come to see her yet? Her heavy stomach crushed the tingles. Maybe Simon didn't want to see her after all. Had he already gone home? A tear trickled down her cheek. The loneliness of the room closed in. Would she ever see him again?

Simon woke with a throbbing headache. No food. No water. And no Fern. How had he let Turner talk him into staying? It wasn't like there was any hope of the challenge continuing, was there? He shook his head, regretting it as soon as his brain sloshed against his skull and sent stabbing pain into his eyeballs. He pressed both hands against his temples and groaned. It had been that one word. Disappointed. No doubt Gregory had coached Turner exactly what to say. Which buttons to jab. No, of course he didn't want Fern to be disappointed in him. No, not his parents either. Not the whole world. Not himself.

Turner had hinted at a touch of promise in the situation. Hadn't he? The pounding in his head was making it hard to keep his thoughts aligned. Something about Gregory coming to see him today. And not giving up hope. Then the sandaled, beach boy had smiled and patted Simon's arm.

"Hello. Permission to enter camp."

Speak of the devil. Simon rotated his head to glance over his shoulder. He felt like an owl eyeballing his prey. As soon as Gregory's face appeared through the dense foliage, the same heat flared in Simon's breast. The same balled fists wished to pound the smug jerk into smithereens.

Gregory emerged, palms out, a neutral look on

his face.

But Simon could see the doubt cross his eyes when their gazes met. "How're your ribs?"

Gregory chuckled. "Um, well, they're sore."

"The next words out of your mouth had better be good news about Fern."

"Yes, yes. Of course. Fern came through surgery well. As soon as the doctor came out of the room, I wanted to fly out and let you know. But I had paperwork and thought it best to wait until this morning. She's expected to make a full recovery."

The breath flew from Simon's lungs. *Thank you, God.* The weight crushing his shoulders flew into the sky on the wings of the next muggy breeze.

"That's what I wanted to talk to you about. May I sit?"

Simon bit his cheek but nodded.

"Remember I said this was a good time to press the limits and learn what can and can't be done?"

"There'd better be an apology coming." Simon popped his knuckles.

"What? Oh, yes. I am so sorry for what has happened to Fern. Of course I am. But that's not what I meant. I think it's time to break some more rules."

Simon quirked his eyebrow. "It's over. Isn't it?"

"No." Gregory sighed. "Listen, everyone thinks I'm out for blood. Out for the most dramatic, audience-appealing craziness I can possibly muster no matter the costs. But that's not it at all. I want you and Fern to succeed."

"Right."

"I'm serious. Just hear me out. I've cut the cameras. This is off the books, as they say. I never wanted you and Fern to give up or get injured. That's why I've been out here watching you in person. It's too hard to judge the body language, the chemistry in the air, if you will, through the camera's lens. I needed to see it. To feel it myself."

How sick was this guy?

"Now, not because I get some kick out of it. But because it helps me plan the right path. The one that will bring you and Fern together as a team the most cohesively."

"You mean to tell me this is all one big, happy team-building exercise?"

"Something like that. But the end goal is so much more. It's life changing."

"Half a million dollars is life changing, all right."

"No." Gregory jumped to his feet and paced next to the dying fire. "That's not what I meant. Can no one see the bigger picture?"

"I guess you'll have to call me blind or stupid. I have no idea what you're getting at."

Gregory grasped Simon by the shoulders and pulled him to his feet. "You said it yourself. You needed redemption. Right?"

"I did."

"Have you found it yet?"

"I don't know."

"How about Fern? What did she need? You've

learned her secrets, I know that. I can tell by the way you look at her. I can tell other things too. Call it a gift, a curse, a blessing. Whatever you name it, I can read people. I've always been able to. That's what makes me so good at my job. My pops has been pushing me my whole life to surrender to his vision for me." Gregory spread his hands wide, like he was reading a giant banner. "Can't you see it? Heir to the most lucrative, soul-crushing business in town."

He wasn't making a lick of sense. Simon thought he'd been the one to hit his head too hard. What was Gregory's excuse for his nuttiness?

"I quit. Dropped the family business like a stone. This," he took in the expanse of the forest with a sweeping arc, "is my future. I've lost the only true love I will ever have. But it's not too late for others."

What was he rambling on about?

"Love, Simon. It's all about love. And I believe you've found it. Haven't you?"

"Let me get this straight. You're saying you sent Fern and me out here so we could almost die together and fall in love?"

Gregory smiled. "Precisely."

"You're crazy!"

"Ah, maybe so. But I can tell by the fuchsia of your cheeks that I'm right. Let me make you a deal. You stay and complete the last remaining test and win the whole shebang for Fern. What is more poetic than that?"

Poetic? Poetic! There was nothing poetic about

Fern lying in a hospital bed, near death, possibly losing an arm. "You really are crazy! I want to see Fern. Now."

Gregory snorted.

Simon raised a balled fist.

"Wait, wait, wait. Just wait. Stay here one more day. Let me talk to Fern. If she says stay, will you listen?"

He dropped his hand to his side. Nodded almost imperceptibly. Gregory had him by the heart again.

Chapter 21

Fern pursed her lips and glared at Gregory. "Did you come to gloat?"

"Not at all. I came to see how you're doing."

He moved like he would sit on the end of her bed. She scooted her foot over to block the empty space and crossed her free arm over the other one resting in a sling across her chest. "I already know I failed. Don't rub it in."

A smile lit up his face. Probably the first genuine one she'd seen from him in weeks. "That's just it, Fern. It's not over."

"What are you talking about? I left. It's over. Your rules. Or have you forgotten the dictionary you had us memorize?"

"Listen, I own the show. I'm the financier, director, editor, and writer. I can do what I please."

Of course he could. He was rich, and he didn't

care what anyone thought about him.

"Hear me out. If you want to kick me out after I'm done, fine. I'll leave and you'll never hear from me again."

Fern's iron grip on her gown loosened. Just a bit.

"I want to let Simon continue. Finish the challenge for both of you."

Her jaw dropped. "Wait. Are you saying Simon is still out there?"

"That's exactly what I'm saying."

Simon hadn't gone home after all. He was still out there. Waiting for her. Keeping his promise to stay no matter what. She flung the blanket off her legs.

"Fern, wait. What are you doing?"

"I'm coming with you." She deftly rolled the knob to close the fluids dripping into her hand, peeled the tape off her skin, and withdrew the IV with her teeth. Pressing a cotton ball she found on the nightstand against the bruised spot, she smiled at Gregory. "Easy peasy."

"You are in absolutely no shape to go traipsing about the forest."

She reached for her bag. Unknotted it with her teeth and her good hand. Managed to free her blue jeans and wrinkled her nose. "Oh my. These. Smell. Awful."

Gregory chuckled for a brief moment and then resumed his frown. "I cannot allow you to do this. It's not safe. You've had major surger—"

"Let me stop you right there. First of all," she

held up her index finger to mark her point, "when did you care about safety?"

"That's not fair."

"Let me finish." She raised her middle finger. "Second of all, you cannot tell me what to do. I knew what I was getting into when I signed on for the show. I will finish it or die trying. Do you understand me?"

His eyebrow quirked, but he kept his mouth shut.

Her ring finger joined the other two already raised. "Third, I refuse to let Simon continue suffering alone." And she couldn't wait to get back to him. He had stayed! After everything, he had stayed. She paused her dressing efforts. "Do you mind?"

Gregory's eyes widened. "Sorry. I'll go find the staff and get your discharge papers." He turned his back.

"No. That will take forever. Give me your shirt."

"My shirt?"

"They cut mine off, remember?"

He unbuttoned his dress shirt and tossed it to her behind his back, leaving him in the dark gray undershirt.

"Thanks." Fern slipped it on and stood. The fluids had done her good. She didn't wobble even a little.

With the sling re-situated around her neck, along with the key on its ribbon, she peeked out of her room door. "All clear. Come on." She tiptoed to the end of the hallway and quietly opened the stairwell door. Her arm didn't hurt at the moment, but how would it feel once the pain meds wore off? It was a chance she was going to have to take. *Lord, thank you for getting me through this injury so far. Please stay with me and get me back to Simon, but most of all, help him.* She padded barefoot downstairs with Gregory's flip-flops echoing behind her. "I need new shoes, Gregory. Can one of your minions meet us at the location with some? And some undergarments?"

"And a shirt. That one cost a hundred and fifty bucks. No way am I letting you mess it up."

Fern giggled. "Fine. Whatever it takes." She had to get back to camp. Anywhere Simon was felt like home. And that's where she wanted to be.

Their return drive to base camp was silent, but Gregory's mind raced. Fern was in no shape to hike into camp. He'd have her flown out. Hang the rules. One of the new assistants met them with his requested supplies. "Thank you, Julia." The brunette flashed him a smile that he'd not soon forget. Would she accept an offer to go to dinner with him? Maybe he'd ask her later. It had been years since he had a date. Was he really ready?

Fern slipped into the nearest empty tent and emerged with a tentative smile. She cradled her arm gently as she slipped the sling around her neck.

Her pain meds must have been wearing off. "Ready?"

She nodded once and made a line toward the forest.

"Fern, wait. You're in no shape to hike—"

"I didn't come back to sit on the sidelines."

"It's your turn to let me finish. I sent the drone out as soon as I knew you were returning. Simon is already on his way to the final clue. We will," he pointed at the chopper, "meet him there."

Her head cocked to one side as she raised an eyebrow and gazed at him for a moment. Sizing him up? A more natural confidence radiated from her. A quiet sort of acceptance of her new strength. His heart filled to overflowing. His pilot season would be a knockout. Even with all the rule-breaking and game-changing.

"Okay. Thank you."

She waited for his assistance to board the helicopter and allowed him to help with her buckle. "You'll be there in less than five minutes. Enjoy the ride!"

"Aren't you coming?"

"Nah. Good luck."

Five minutes? She took a deep breath. Only five minutes away from Simon. Who had probably had to hike and totally exhaust himself to get there. Five minutes until she could rush from this metal beast and . . . And what? Nuzzle into his chest and listen to the steady beat of his heart? Wrap her one good arm around his slender waist and stay there until the sun went down? Run her fingers through his scruffy beard and pull his face to hers? She shook her head and swiped her palm down her thigh.

Her heart pounded as the helicopter circled a clearing and the pilot prepared to land. Where was he? No sign of his tall form anywhere in sight. Maybe he hadn't made it yet?

She ducked under the whipping blades and ran for the run-down cabin at the edge of the meadow. When the helicopter lifted and disappeared over the trees, she could hear herself think. How long had she been in the hospital? Could it be only one day? She hugged her injured arm closer. Surrounded by technology, comforts, and people, she'd been so confident. So sure this was a good idea. What if her bandage got wet and set up an infection? What if she started bleeding again? What if—

"Fern?"

She spun on her heels.

Simon entered the glade with his mouth gaping open. "What are you doing here?"

"I . . . I couldn't let you finish alone."

He stopped a few feet away and labored to catch his breath.

How she longed to race into his arms. But what would he think? Would he raise his to return her embrace? Her heart beat at her ribcage, trying to run to him without her. "I was worried about you. Out here all alone with no one to boss you around."

His smile broke through the brown beard, lighting his eyes. "You were worried about me?"

"Yeah. You know you need me. Don't you know everything stops turning unless I'm there to make sure it works?"

He chortled. "Trust me, I haven't forgotten." He closed the gap between them.

Why wouldn't her lungs work? She gazed into his down-turned face. Fluttering wings bubbled in her belly, pulsing shockwaves through her whole body. She rose onto her tiptoes and let her fingers graze his cheek, run deep into the fluff at his jawline.

In one swift motion, he circled her waist and pulled her body close to his.

How she'd missed that spot where her shoulders fit perfectly within the frame of his arms. The hard muscles of his chest flexing beneath.

"I missed you."

"I missed you too." She placed her hand behind his neck and hid her face in the dip at its base, nestling in under his chin. His chest vibrated beneath her ear, thudding with the stampeding of his heartbeat. She smiled. "You're dehydrated."

His deep voice echoed in his chest. "Nonsense. I'm in love."

In love. With her. He hadn't changed his mind? After everything he knew about her and everything they'd been through. "We have work to do. Tell me that again when you are well-fed and well-rested. And not dehydrated."

He pulled away, grasped her chin, and tilted her face toward his. "Listen to me, Fern. Nothing is going to change after we go home. Not on my end."

"I believe you believe that."

"I bet ya a steak and potato dinner." He grinned ear to ear.

"Those are high *steaks*, mister."

His laughter resounded through the glade. "So spunky with your new fluids and someone else's blood. You wait and see, Dr. Strongbow. Now," he grabbed her by the hand, "Let's find the treasure at the end of this ridiculous rainbow."

"I don't see any rainbows." Just a few stars.

"We should split up." Fern's voice echoed down the stairs from the loft of the old cabin.

"Huh-uh. I'm not letting you out of my sight."

"You can't see me right now."

She had a good point. He took the rickety steps two at a time. Planted his hands on his hips and grinned. "Can now."

Her musical laugh filled the small space. "Oh boy. The treasure has to be here somewhere, right?"

"This last clue only told me the direction to hike. I guess this is why he didn't want us outside the pink flags very often, eh? Afraid we'd stumble on this little gem and find the treasure before he had a real chance to murder us." He waggled his eyebrows, which earned him the smile he'd hoped for. "But I assume since Gregory flew you out here it must be nearby." They'd searched the sparsely filled cabin for any tiny cracks, hidden spaces, or extra clues and had seen nothing. "Come on. Let's try the barn." He held out his hand, and she took it without hesitation. Could he hold onto her slender fingers until the end of time? Better yet, hold her entire body in his arms and never let go? His heart skipped a beat. He needed to focus.

"Let's think about the clues we've had."

"Okay."

"There have been two truths, right?"

"Right."

"We've hiked to the waterfall for supplies, but there was nothing special about that. You don't think I missed something do you?"

He bit his lip. "No. I think Gregory would've made us wait for the next clue if we had."

"Yes, good point. We've rappelled down the cliff."

"We've?" He nudged her with his elbow.

Her cheeks flushed crimson. "You know what I mean. We've shot at little bags with a bow and arrows."

"What was in those bags anyway?"

"Letters, remember?" She snapped. "Oh, and the flashlight and pocketknife."

He pulled her to a stop and motioned for her to wait. "I'll take a look."

The lopsided barn leaned hard to the west. What was holding the old boards up? Inside, the smell of mold and mildew assailed his nostrils.

"Kind of hard to see!" he shouted over his shoulder. He pulled the little flashlight free and shone it into the cobwebbed stalls one by one. All eight of them were empty. The ladder to the loft no longer held any rungs. Surely Gregory wouldn't have put something up there. Not without a clue or a rope or some dangerous method for getting into the top of the barn. He chuckled. They'd been blessed to survive the challenges they'd been through thus far. *Please don't take us out on the last one, Gregory.*

"See anything?"

"Nope. Hang on a sec. I'm coming out." He picked his way back through the webs and leftover straw. "Whew! It's a mess in there."

"No luck?"

"Nada. What are we missing?"

They both searched the field. He noticed the cameras lodged in the trees and on the sides of the buildings for the first time and chuckled.

"What?"

"I can't believe I've gotten so used to being on film I don't even notice them anymore."

Fern trailed the length of his arm and waved at the nearest camera. "Me neither. Never thought that would happen."

Simon resisted the urge to pull Fern close to his side by crossing his arms over his chest and concentrating on the puzzle before them. Gregory had been so cunning and intelligent so far. He wouldn't hide the treasure somewhere simple. "Wasn't there sand or something in the bags too?"

"Huh? Oh, yeah. One had sand. One had river rock. Why?"

"I was thinking. None of the things Gregory has done have been without a point. Maybe those are significant too." That was it. "I've got it." The pride beaming from her eyes, directed at him, made his heart sing. "What would a homestead use sand and river rock in?" He raised his eyebrows.

Comprehension dawned across her face. "A spring house."

"Bingo."

"Did you see a creek as you hiked in?"

"No. You see anything flying in?" He winked.

Tingles zinged through her chest. "It's not my fault Gregory went all soft and decided to give me a break. I almost died. Remember?"

His smile fell. "You're right. I'm sorry."

"I'm teasing you, Simon." She touched his forearm and rubbed her thumb across the prominent tendons and veins. "There has to be a water source close. No homesteader would have built here without one."

"That's what they spelled, you know."

"What what spelled?"

"The letters. They spelled homestead." His chest puffed. "Figured it out all on my own."

"I'm proud of you." And she really was. He'd been the most supportive, most wonderful partner she didn't even know to dream of. Her first impressions had been so wrong. Marred by her own negativity and fear.

This was the last clue. She stopped in her tracks. It was almost over. What would happen afterward? She'd have new riches, and so would Simon. Even if he did love her as he said, he only knew her in one environment. What happened when the stress of the real world came back into sharp focus? When the people who were parts of their individual lives surrounded them once more?

"Hey, what's wrong?" Concern wrinkled his brow as he peered down at her.

His lips, so close above hers, turned up at the corners. He leaned closer. So near that each quick puff of breath brushed against her face.

Her words came out as a breathy whisper. "What's next?"

His warm mouth covered hers, his lips melting against her flesh. She drew in a sharp breath and let her eyelids fall closed. Let the hot spikes of adrenaline course through her stomach. This was not what she meant. But it sure was nice. All thoughts of cameras and game shows, treasure boxes and the key around her neck, her injured arm and his depleted body rushed away with the quickening of her heartbeat.

When Simon pulled away, she nearly fell, so oblivious was she to every other thing besides his arms around her and his lips gently touching hers. He chuckled, and she slapped his arm, but when he turned, her fingers flew to her tingling lips.

He grabbed her hand and tugged. "Come on. I think I hear water."

She followed his lead farther into the trees. "Simon, look."

"That's got to be it."

They knelt before a partially collapsed, moss-shingled roof barely clinging to the top of two cinder block walls. They projected parallel to one another from a steep bank. A narrow, clear stream of water gurgled from within and trailed deeper into the forest.

Simon moved around to the front and looked inside. He scooped a handful and held it for her to see. "River rocks and sand. I think we've found it."

"I've never seen one quite like this before. Have you?"

"I'm definitely not a spring house expert."

She laughed. "Neither am I, but usually they are a small room with shelves on either side. This one looks like it goes pretty far back. Do you think it's safe?"

"Only one way to find out."

"I hate it when you say that."

He grinned. "Be back in a jiffy."

Sara L. Foust

Chapter 22

Fern rolled her shoulders to stretch out the kinks and the worry gnawing at her insides as soon as Simon's backside disappeared from view. If she leaned her head into the short opening, she could hear the sounds of his footsteps, occasional scrapings she presumed were his clothing brushing the walls, and the water steadily trickling between her feet. She tapped her fingers over the elbow buried beneath layers of bandages. "Simon?" she yelled.

A muffled response echoed from within that she couldn't quite make out. He sounded okay, though. Right?

Her left foot bounced. Kicked a rock. Still Simon didn't appear. Her worry didn't make her feel any better either. Imagine that. *Lord, please watch over him in there. We've had enough close calls to last a lifetime. I don't know what I'd do if I lost him.*

She cocked her head to one side and brought her finger to her lips. Yes. The prayer and thought in one was true. She couldn't imagine life without Simon in it. Was that what it meant to be in love? Or maybe it was the thrilling shiver sent coursing through her every atom by his kiss. Her heart fluttered. That kiss. Those lips. She could have stayed pressed against them forever. Could have enjoyed the warmth spreading through her like sunshine after a snowstorm for every minute of every day.

If she had been holding anything, she would have dropped it. She plopped onto the ground. She loved him. She loved Simon. And he said he loved her, but what if he changed his mind? Why couldn't her realization have stayed hidden? If he recanted his declaration once this was over, would she ever be able to recover?

The subtle sound of grating or sliding broke into her thoughts. She peered into the cave-like spring house filled with an onyx so thick it was like a wall. "Simon!" This time there was no answer. Fern jumped into the water and took two steps into the sheltered recess. "Simon!" Nothing. The water beneath her slowed to a crawl. No. That couldn't be a good sign.

Groping through the pitch-black, Fern used her one free hand to ward off falling. Something was wrong. Had there been a cave-in of some sort? If Simon's exit was blocked, so was the water's. Her heart sped, and her mouth went dry. *Please, Lord. Help me!* Simon had the only flashlight, and she had a gimp arm. How would she find him? And if she did, how would she save him?

The GoPro. Of course! She yanked it from her back pocket, switched it to night vision mode, and watched through the screen as she made slow progress into the tunnel. It seemed that the creators of the spring house had utilized a natural cave, walled in the entrance, and added wooden braces in the weak places much like a coal mine. The tiny dot of light from the entrance faded to a pinpoint. "Simon!" Her voice bounced back to her ears from a wall directly in her path.

"Fern! I'm here!"

She placed her hand on the dirt blocking her from Simon. "Hang on, I'm gonna get you out. Are you okay?"

"I'm okay. I found it! I found the prize!"

A grin stretched across her face. He was stuck in an underground tomb filling with spring water, but his excitement for the prize filled the space with exuberance rather than fear. She glanced around her feet, pulling a broken shaft of board free from the rubble. *Lord, I need some more help here. If I dig and it all collapses again . . . Just, please, keep it stable long enough to get him out of there.* With all the power she could muster, she attacked the mud and rocks before her. When she paused for breath, she heard the sounds of Simon digging from his side too. "Are you still okay?"

"Right as rain."

"I love you, Simon."

Had he heard her? His silence lasted so long, she started to say it again. Had something happened? Was he conscious? Had his heart already changed at the sight of the prize money and the knowledge it was all over and they were going home?

"Simon?" Her stick broke through the dirt wall and was yanked from her hand.

Simon emerged, breaking through the hole in one last lunge. Mud-covered from head-to-toe and illuminated by the single flashlight beam, he was quite a sight. "It's about time." He scooped her trembling frame close and pressed his lips to hers.

Fern couldn't breathe. Didn't want to even. Nothing mattered but Simon's warm, slightly muddy lips against hers.

He pulled away, disappeared into the far chamber, and emerged carrying a hard-sided, green suitcase. And the biggest grin she'd ever seen shining from under the mud and his messy beard. "We did it!"

"And I have the key." She touched the ribbon around her neck and smiled.

Six Months Later

"Hey, Fern. Come check this out."

She laid the spatula next to the pan of frying

onions and garlic and wiped her hands on a towel. "Your mom called again this morning. She reminded me of the family dinner this weekend," she said as she walked into the living room where Simon perched on the edge of their couch.

"Okay, good."

He obviously wasn't fully listening, but she doubted he had forgotten. The invitation, and more than that, the spirit in which it was given, had made his chest swell and his shoulders stand tall. The rift between Simon and his family was mending. She kissed his cheek. "Did you hear back from your brother?"

"Huh? Oh, yes. Lance is doing well. Only a few more weeks in rehab and he will be released. He's excited about his cabin. That was a wonderful idea." He pulled her to his hip. Having Lance nearby for support would be what Simon and his younger brother needed to repair all the years of pain.

Simon kissed her shoulder. "But that's not what I meant. Look, we're famous." He pressed play on the DVR remote.

Fern started to giggle but realized he wasn't joking.

The reporter on the evening news smiled and began the next segment. "Survival Tennessee's first contestants, Simon Fincuff and Dr. Fern Strongbow, were married over the weekend at a small ceremony on their homestead. Simon and Fern were the 'trial and error phase' contestants, the show's creator and producer, Gregory Vanderbilt the third, told reporter Allan Leslie in a recent interview."

The clip cut to a video of Gregory chatting with the news reporter while overseeing construction of the show's new base camp cabins. The new assistant who had so kindly given Fern replacement clothes after the hospital, stood proudly at his side, her hand tucked into his. Good for Gregory.

"I'm tickled to death that Simon and Fern made it through the first season. They performed above and beyond what I expected, and they paved the way for the show's second season, featuring two brand-new East Tennessee natives."

The news anchor's smiling face appeared again as she continued, "Dr. Strongbow has purchased a veterinary clinic near their new hometown and vowed to help homesteaders who can't afford expensive care take care of the animals that are so vital to their farms' success."

Simon swept her up in a hug, lifting her feet from the ground and twirling her round and round until her head spun. "What do you know about that?"

Fern laughed and pressed her hands to his cheeks. "I especially like that part about us being married." Her cheeks flushed hot at the hungry look in his eyes.

"Me too."

He crushed her tighter and pressed his sweet lips to hers. The wave of heat left her cheeks and cascaded over her, all the way to the tips of her toes. As they fell onto the couch together, Fern pulled away. "We have work to do, mister. This honeymooning on our new homestead was supposed to be a working vacation." She swatted his shoulder when he frowned. "And my dinner's burning."

"I like the honeymooning part better." He kissed her again, threatening all resolve to resist him. Between the kisses he planted on her neck, he spoke breathy, broken words. "I. Love. You. Mrs. Fincuff."

She pressed her lips to his ear and whispered, "I love you, too, Mr. Fincuff."

A moan rumbled from deep in his chest.

The onions and garlic burned in their buttery frying pan, but it didn't matter. She had everything she needed wrapped in her arms. Their new farm, situated smackdab in the middle of 300 pristine acres, was just the icing on the cake.

We are bound to thank God always for you, brethren, as it is meet, because that your faith groweth exceedingly, and the charity of every one of you all toward each other aboundeth.
II Thessalonians 1:3

A Special Note from the Author

Dear Reader,

Thank you so much for reading the third and final installment in the Love, Hope, and Faith Series. I pray that Fern and Simon's stories blessed you. I would be forever grateful if you would take the time to leave honest reviews. As always, I love hearing from readers. If you have any questions, concerns, or prayer requests, please feel free to contact me through my website (listed below).

If you haven't yet read *Callum's Compass* and *Camp Hope* (books one and two in this series), it isn't too late! All three novels in the Love, Hope, and Faith Series read well as standalone novels. You can find them wherever books are sold.

I have many more future projects in the works and would love to be able to keep you in the loop about them. You can join my email friends to get updates and special bonuses (like a free digital scrapbook about the real-life places that inspired scenes in *Callum's Compass*!) right to your inbox. Sign up at www.saralfoust.com.

Thank you for sharing this journey with me,

Sara L. Foust

Sara L. Foust

Acknowledgments

I am so thankful for my family. They have encouraged me, purchased a gazillion copies of my books, told their friends about my writing, and supported me in every moment.

Thank you to the entire team at Mantle Rock Publishing for giving me a solid start in this wonderful writing business.

Thank you to my bestie Becky for reading the early draft and giving me invaluable feedback.

Thank you to my other bestie Becky for talking all things books and writing with me.

Thank you to my readers. Without you, I would have no audience. I hope, beyond any other thing, that you have been blessed, encouraged, and found healing in the words God has given me.

I am, above all, thankful God granted me the passion and ability to write for Him. It is truly a wonderful calling.

About the Author

Sara is a multi-published, award-winning author, freelance editor, owner of Silver Lining Literary Services, LLC, and mother of five who writes surrounded by the beauty of East Tennessee. She earned her bachelor's degree in Animal Science from the University of Tennessee and is a member of American Christian Fiction Writers, The Christian PEN, and Sigma Tau Delta English Honor Society. Sara finds inspiration in her faith, her family, and the beauty of nature. When she isn't writing, you can find her reading, camping, and spending time outdoors. To learn more about her and her work or to become a part of her email friend's group, please visit www.saralfoust.com.

Find Sara at:
www.saralfoust.com

Also by Sara L. Foust

Kat Williams's brother died in a gruesome accident in the mountains of East Tennessee. She blames herself.

Ryan Jenkins's fiancée was murdered. He couldn't protect her.

With the death of her brother, Kat believes she is unworthy of love from anyone—even God. When a good friend elicits a promise that she will stop living in the past, then leaves her clues to a real-life treasure hunt, Kat embarks on an adventure chock-full of danger. To find the treasure, Kat will have to survive wild animals—and even wilder men. Can she rely on Ryan, the handsome wildlife officer assigned to protect her…without falling in love?

Ryan swore off love when his fiancée was murdered, but feelings long buried rise to the surface around Kat. He volunteers to help with her treasure hunt, vowing to keep her safe. Together they venture deep into caves and tunnels…and even deeper into the depths of their unplumbed hearts.

➤

Amy Dawson directs a summer camp for foster children near Briceville, Tennessee. A foster mom for the first time, her responsibilities as mother to a traumatized child bring a whole new set of challenges and joys.

But when Amy's four-year-old foster daughter is dragged into the mountains of Royal Blue by a former employee, parenting challenges are overshadowed by a new nightmare. The Sheriff's department fails to procure viable leads, and Amy can't sit idle. Her childhood friend and first love, Jack Evans, returns to lend his skills as tracker. Problem is, he also stirs up romantic memories Amy would rather leave buried.

Jack struggles to let go of his past failures and prove his reliability by bringing Mattie home, but fears when he left camp nineteen years ago and failed to keep a promise to Amy he permanently lost her confidence.

As Amy plunges into the wilderness on horseback to search for Mattie, she must decide who she trusts, let go of her childhood traumas, and learn to rely on hope in God. Facing dehydration, starvation, and a convoluted kidnapper, will she succeed in recovering her precious foster daughter or get lost in the vast wilderness forever?

Did you enjoy the Love, Hope, and Faith Series?
My Smoky Mountain Suspense Series is set right here
in the Great Smoky Mountains of East Tennessee, and
I would love to have you check it out!

She lives in a utopian town, where nothing bad ever happens...But when officers Zachary Leebow and Annalise Baker are invited to join a new special-task team, the Smoky Mountain Investigative Force, their lives become even more intertwined than before. With everything around them changing and an unnamed body on their hands, they must decipher the clues to their individual cases......before kidnapping turns into murder.

She is looking forward to a new beginning in a new town...Until an old case heats up again and a familiar face brings the past back to life. Recently recruited Special Agents Annalise Baker and Zachary Leebow are called upon to investigate major crimes in the Great Smoky Mountains. Now, with a missing woman that seems a bit too familiar and a suspected traitor in their midst, these best friends are not only tasked with solving a puzzling disappearance......but fighting for their own lives.

When an unreliable witness reports a body that they can't find...Special Agents Annalise Baker and Zachary Leebow will be stretched to their physical and emotional limits, testing not only their tenuous new relationship but their faith too. Deep in the wilderness near Cades Cove, Tennessee, the Smoky Mountain Investigative Force's spotless track record is on the line if they fail. ...But how do they solve a crime when there is no victim?

Murder reaches too close to home this time...When Smoky Mountain Investigative Force's lead agent, Kirk Johnson, is slain, Special Agents Annalise Baker and Zachary Leebow are forced to face and solve a crime they never anticipated...With an outcome no one sees coming.

Available Now!